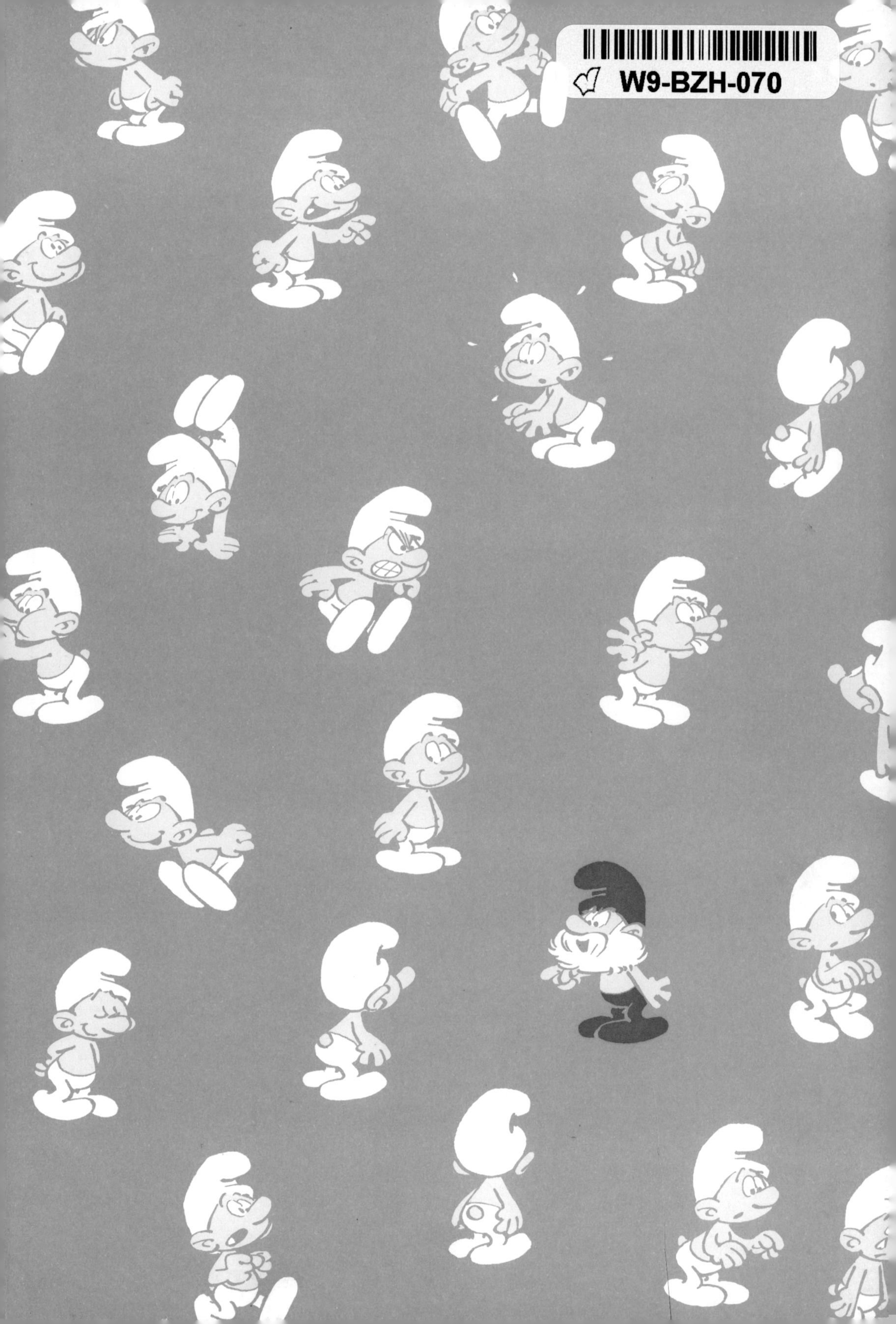

THE ASTROSMURF ★★

Peyo

THE ASTRO SMURF

That's one small step for a smurf...
...one giant leap for Smurfkind! This is the best smurf of my life!
You know, I wonder if this planet is inhabited?
KAYAAA! KAYAAA!
IT IS!

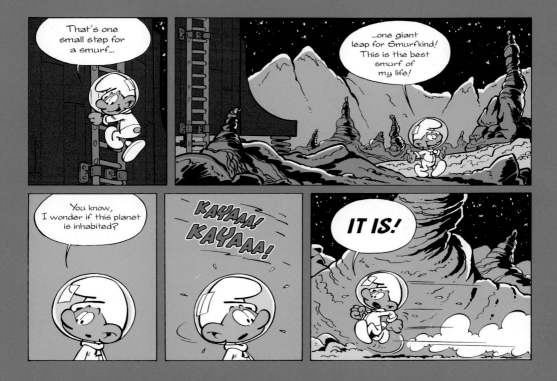

A SMURFS GRAPHIC NOVEL BY PEYO

PAPERCUTZ™
NEW YORK

SMURFS GRAPHIC NOVELS AVAILABLE FROM PAPERCUTZ™

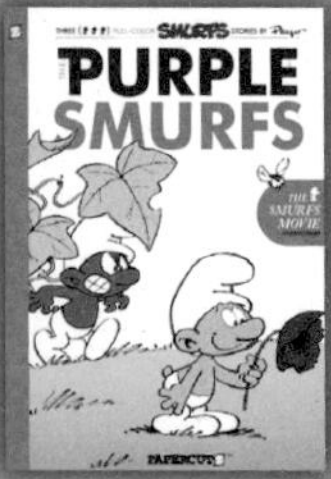
PURPLE SMURFS
PAPERCUTZ
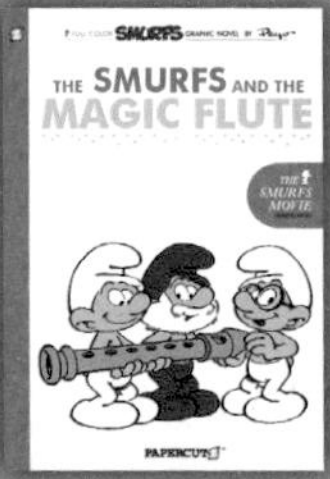
THE SMURFS AND THE MAGIC FLUTE
PAPERCUTZ
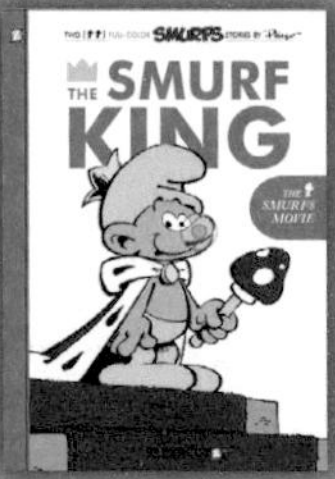
THE SMURF KING
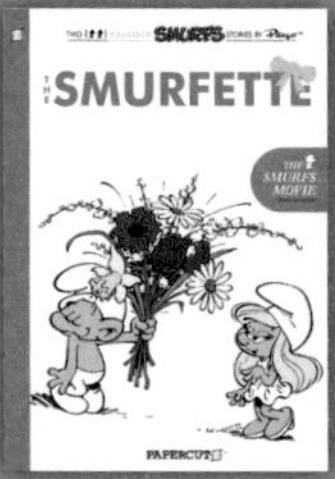
THE SMURFETTE
PAPERCUTZ
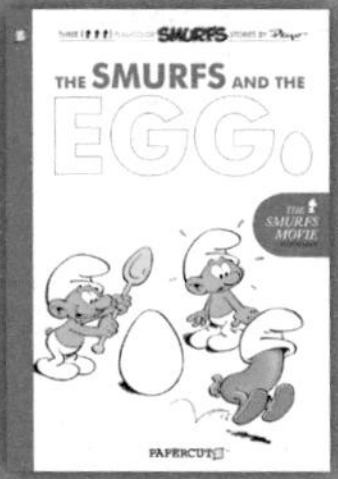
THE SMURFS AND THE EGG
PAPERCUTZ
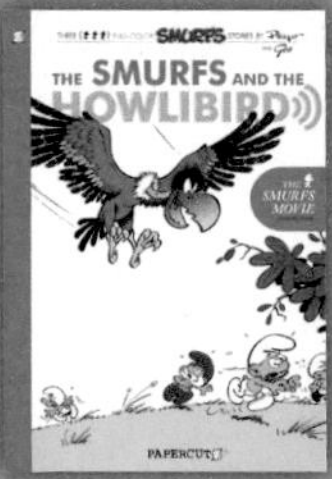
THE SMURFS AND THE HOWLIBIRD
PAPERCUTZ

1. **THE PURPLE SMURFS**
2. **THE SMURFS AND THE MAGIC FLUTE**
3. **THE SMURF KING**
4. **THE SMURFETTE**
5. **THE SMURFS AND THE EGG**
6. **THE SMURFS AND THE HOWLIBIRD**
7. **THE ASTROSMURF**

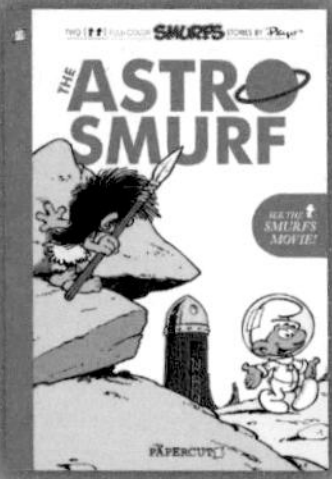
THE ASTRO SMURF
PAPERCUTZ

COMING SOON:

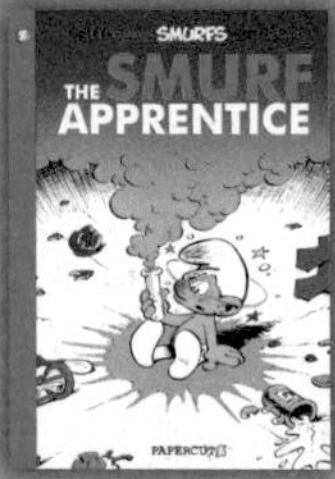
THE SMURF APPRENTICE
PAPERCUTZ
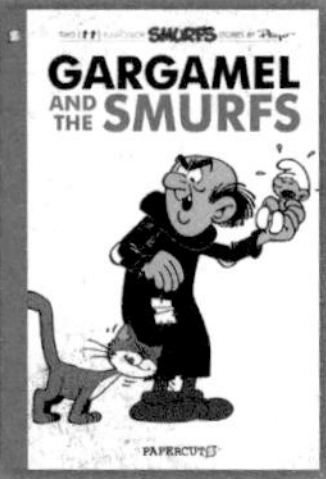
GARGAMEL AND THE SMURFS
PAPERCUTZ

8. **THE SMURF APPRENTICE**
9. **GARGAMEL AND THE SMURFS**

The Smurfs graphic novels are available in paperback for $5.99 each and in hardcover for $10.99 each at booksellers everywhere.

Or order through us. Please add $4.00 for postage and handling for the first book, add $1.00 for each additional book. Please make check payable to NBM Publishing. Send to: PAPERCUTZ, 40 Exchange Place Suite 1308, New York, NY 10005 (1-800-886-1223).

WWW.PAPERCUTZ.COM

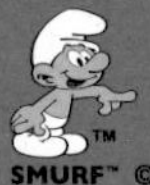

THE ASTROSMURF

"The Astrosmurf"
BY PEYO

"The Smurf Submarine"
BY PEYO

Joe Johnson, *SMURFLATIONS*
Adam Grano, *SMURFIC DESIGN*
Janice Chiang, *LETTERING SMURFETTE*
Matt. Murray, *SMURF CONSULTANT*
Michael Petranek, *ASSOCIATE SMURF*
Jim Salicrup, *SMURF-IN-CHIEF*

PAPERBACK EDITION ISBN: 978-1-59707-250-2
HARDCOVER EDITION ISBN: 978-1-59707-251-9

PRINTED IN CHINA APRIL 2011 BY WKT CO. LTD.
3/F PHASE I LEADER INDUSTRIAL CENTRE
188 TEXACO ROAD, TSEUN WAN, N.T., HONG KONG

DISTRIBUTED BY MACMILLAN
FIRST PAPERCUTZ PRINTING

THE ASTROSMURF

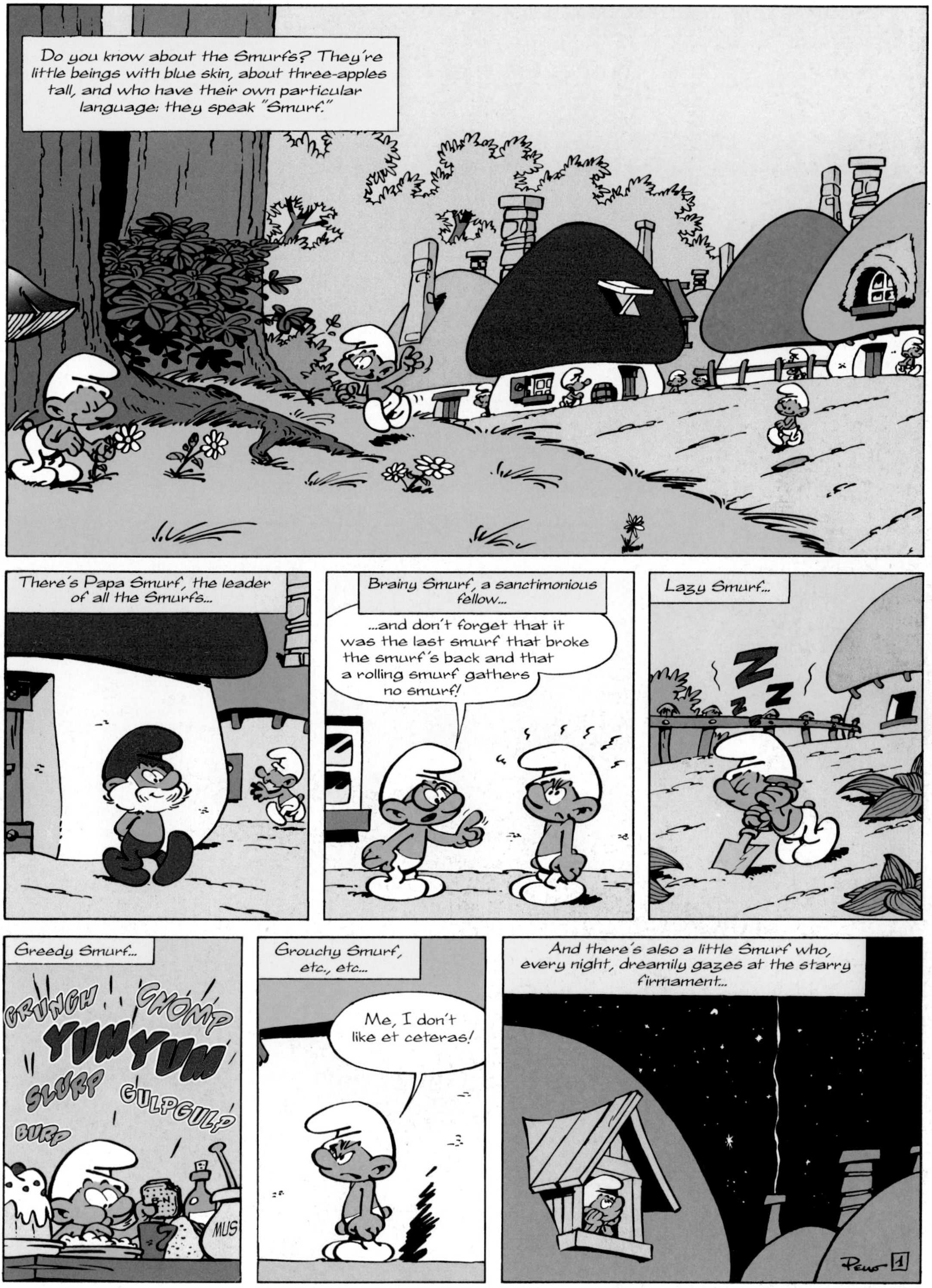

Do you know about the Smurfs? They're little beings with blue skin, about three-apples tall, and who have their own particular language: they speak "Smurf."
There's Papa Smurf, the leader of all the Smurfs...
Brainy Smurf, a sanctimonious fellow...
...and don't forget that it was the last smurf that broke the smurf's back and that a rolling smurf gathers no smurf!
Lazy Smurf...
Z Z Z
Greedy Smurf...
CRUNCH
CHOMP
YUM YUM
SLURP
GULPGULP
BURP
MUS
Grouchy Smurf, etc., etc...
Me, I don't like et ceteras!
And there's also a little Smurf who, every night, dreamily gazes at the starry firmament...
Peyo
1

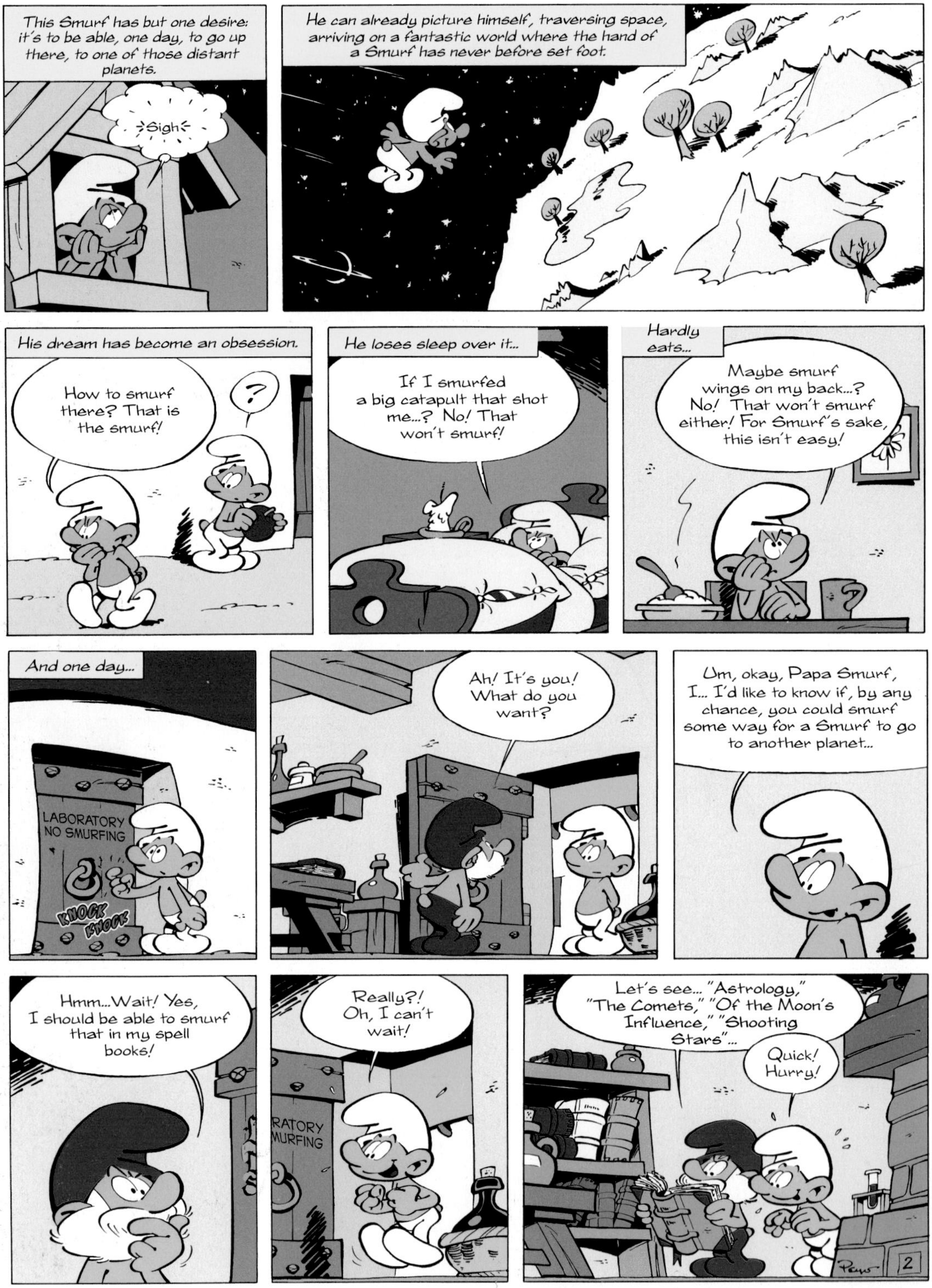

This Smurf has but one desire: it's to be able, one day, to go up there, to one of those distant planets.
Sigh
He can already picture himself, traversing space, arriving on a fantastic world where the hand of a Smurf has never before set foot.
His dream has become an obsession.
How to smurf there? That is the smurf!
?
He loses sleep over it...
If I smurfed a big catapult that shot me...? No! That won't smurf!
Hardly eats...
Maybe smurf wings on my back...? No! That won't smurf either! For Smurf's sake, this isn't easy!
And one day...
LABORATORY NO SMURFING
KNOCK KNOCK
Ah! It's you! What do you want?
Um, okay, Papa Smurf, I... I'd like to know if, by any chance, you could smurf some way for a Smurf to go to another planet...
Hmm...Wait! Yes, I should be able to smurf that in my spell books!
Really?! Oh, I can't wait!
RATORY
MURFING
Let's see... "Astrology," "The Comets," "Of the Moon's Influence," "Shooting Stars"...
Quick! Hurry!
2

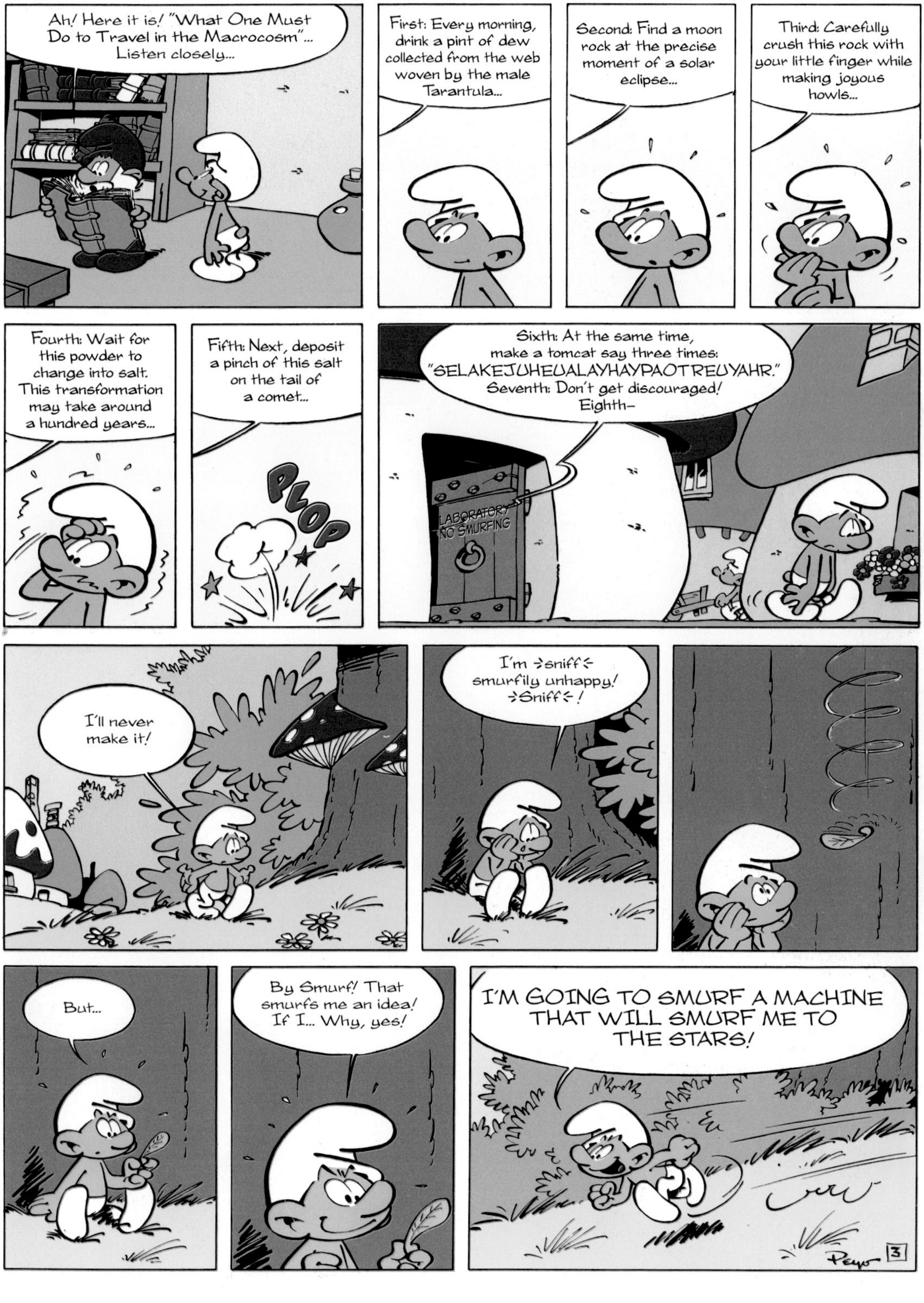

Ah! Here it is! "What One Must Do to Travel in the Macrocosm"... Listen closely...
First: Every morning, drink a pint of dew collected from the web woven by the male Tarantula...
Second: Find a moon rock at the precise moment of a solar eclipse...
Third: Carefully crush this rock with your little finger while making joyous howls...
Fourth: Wait for this powder to change into salt. This transformation may take around a hundred years...
Fifth: Next, deposit a pinch of this salt on the tail of a comet...
PLOP
Sixth: At the same time, make a tomcat say three times: "SELAKEJUHEUALAYHAYPAOTREUYAHR." Seventh: Don't get discouraged! Eighth–
LABORATORY NO SMURFING
I'll never make it!
I'm ≻sniff≺ smurfily unhappy! ≻Sniff≺!
But...
By Smurf! That smurfs me an idea! If I... Why, yes!
I'M GOING TO SMURF A MACHINE THAT WILL SMURF ME TO THE STARS!
Peyo
3

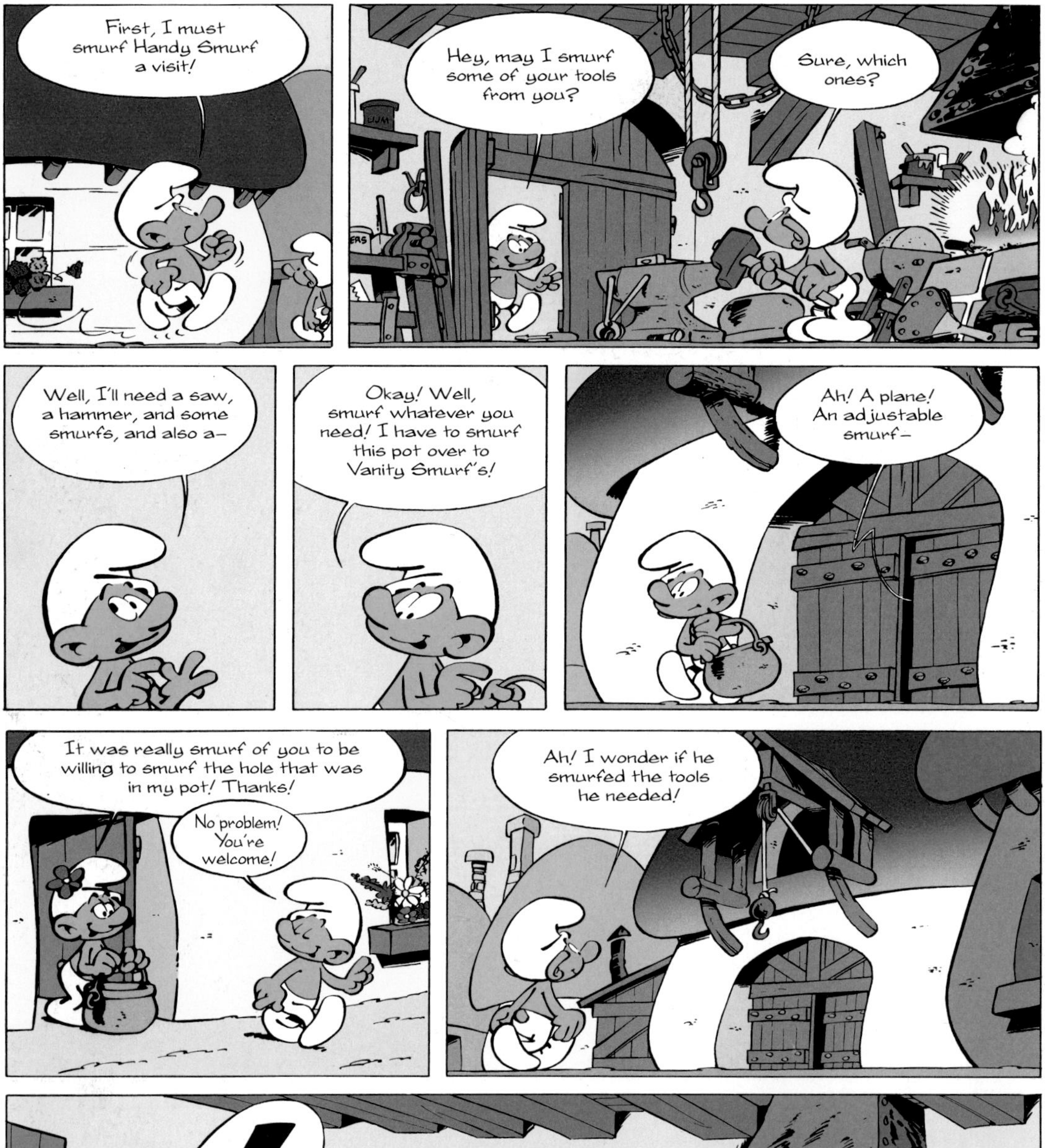
First, I must smurf Handy Smurf a visit!
Hey, may I smurf some of your tools from you?
Sure, which ones?
Well, I'll need a saw, a hammer, and some smurfs, and also a–
Okay! Well, smurf whatever you need! I have to smurf this pot over to Vanity Smurf's!
Ah! A plane! An adjustable smurf–
It was really smurf of you to be willing to smurf the hole that was in my pot! Thanks!
No problem! You're welcome!
Ah! I wonder if he smurfed the tools he needed!
!
4
Peyo

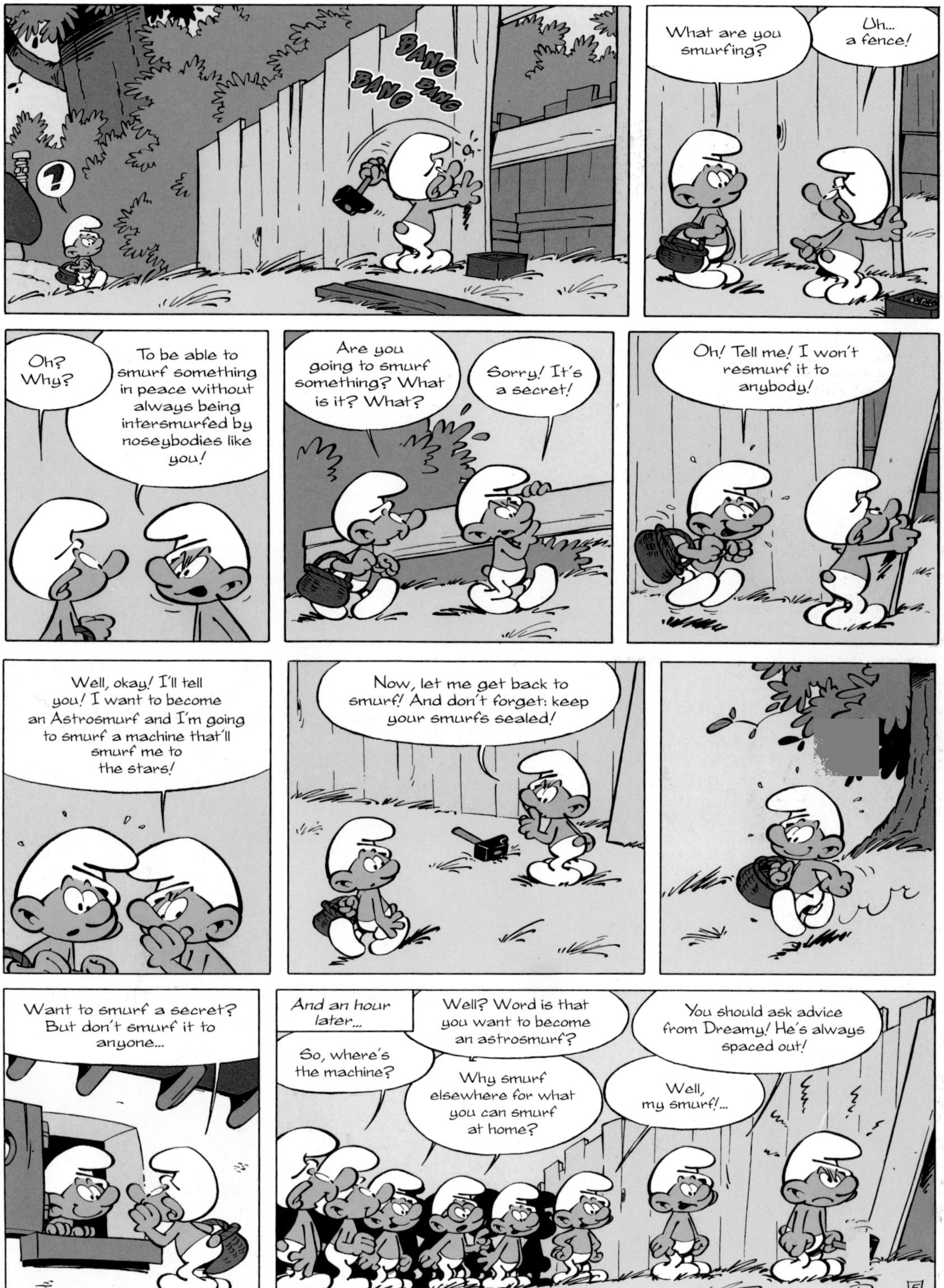
BANG
BANG
BANG
?
What are you smurfing?
Uh... a fence!
Oh? Why?
To be able to smurf something in peace without always being intersmurfed by noseybodies like you!
Are you going to smurf something? What is it? What?
Sorry! It's a secret!
Oh! Tell me! I won't resmurf it to anybody!
Well, okay! I'll tell you! I want to become an Astrosmurf and I'm going to smurf a machine that'll smurf me to the stars!
Now, let me get back to smurf! And don't forget: keep your smurfs sealed!
Want to smurf a secret? But don't smurf it to anyone...
And an hour later...
Well? Word is that you want to become an astrosmurf?
So, where's the machine?
Why smurf elsewhere for what you can smurf at home?
You should ask advice from Dreamy! He's always spaced out!
Well, my smurf!...
Peyo
5

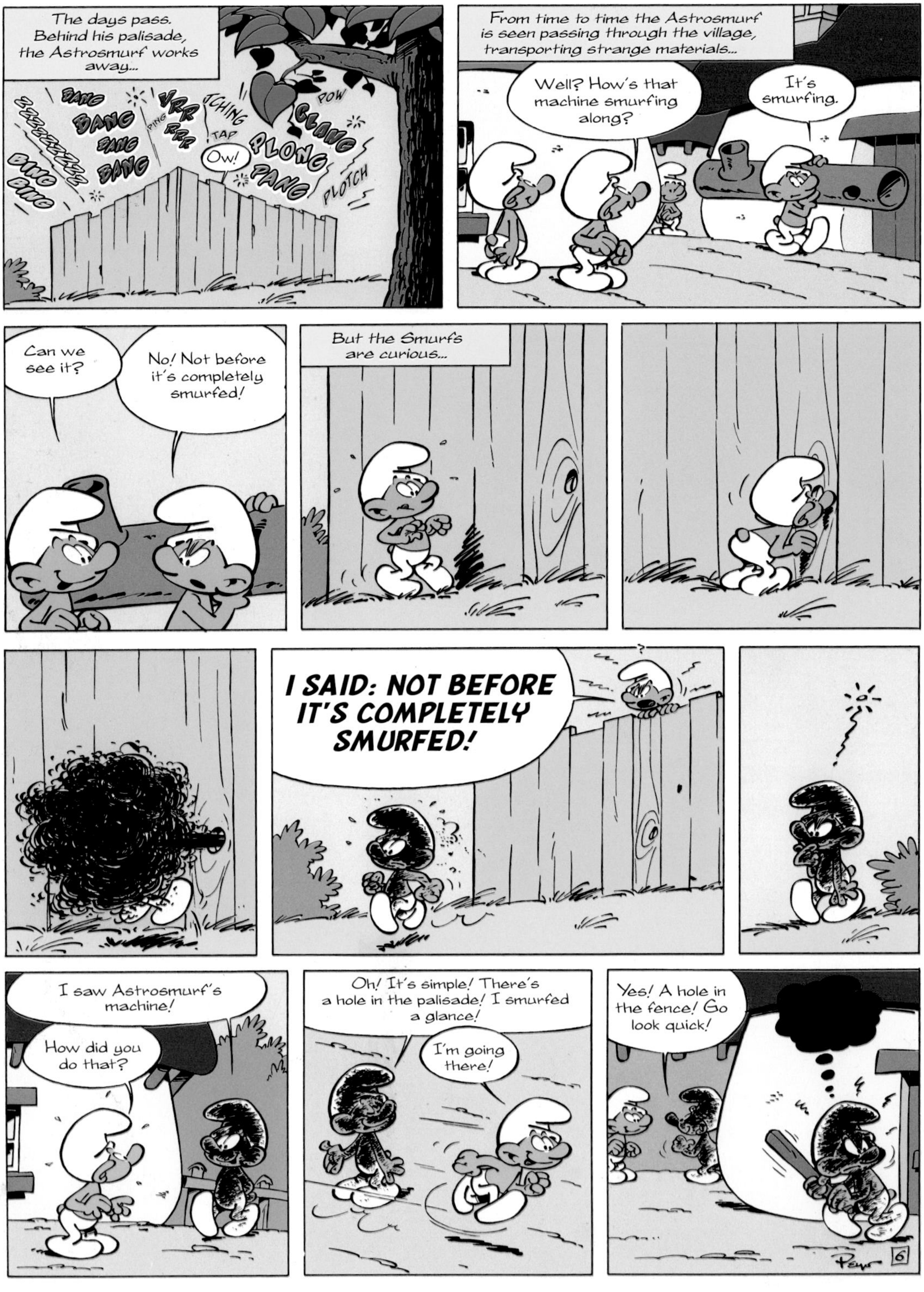
The days pass. Behind his palisade, the Astrosmurf works away...
BANG
BANG
BANG
BANG
VRR RRR
PING
TCHING
TAP
Ow!
POW
CLANG
PLONG
PANG
PLOTCH
From time to time the Astrosmurf is seen passing through the village, transporting strange materials...
Well? How's that machine smurfing along?
It's smurfing.
Can we see it?
No! Not before it's completely smurfed!
But the Smurfs are curious...
I SAID: NOT BEFORE IT'S COMPLETELY SMURFED!
I saw Astrosmurf's machine!
How did you do that?
Oh! It's simple! There's a hole in the palisade! I smurfed a glance!
I'm going there!
Yes! A hole in the fence! Go look quick!
Peyo
6

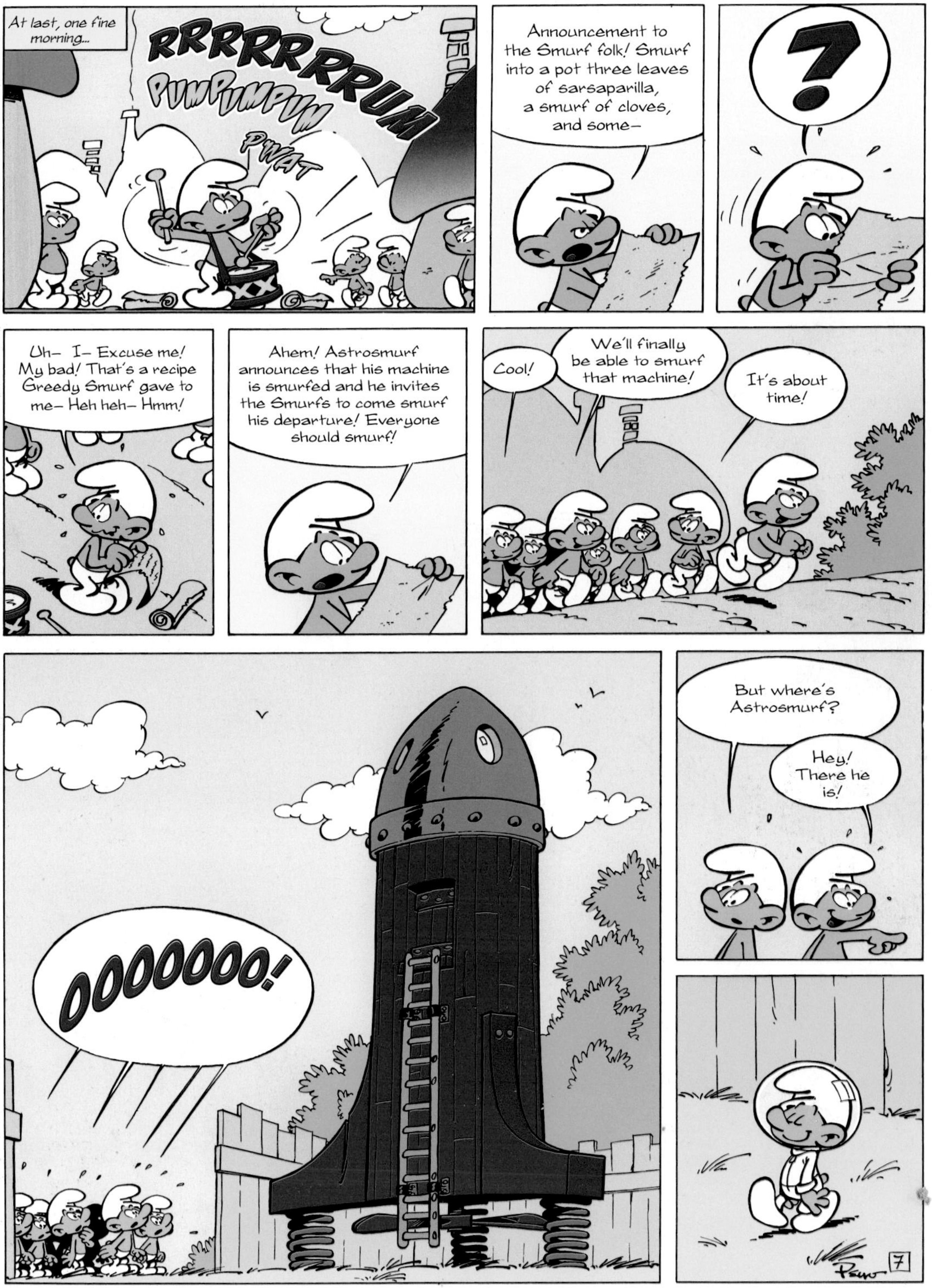
At last, one fine morning...
RRRRRRRRUM
PUMPUMPUMPUM
PWAT
Announcement to the Smurf folk! Smurf into a pot three leaves of sarsaparilla, a smurf of cloves, and some–
?
Uh– I– Excuse me! My bad! That's a recipe Greedy Smurf gave to me– Heh heh– Hmm!
Ahem! Astrosmurf announces that his machine is smurfed and he invites the Smurfs to come smurf his departure! Everyone should smurf!
Cool!
We'll finally be able to smurf that machine!
It's about time!
OOOOOOO!
But where's Astrosmurf?
Hey! There he is!
7

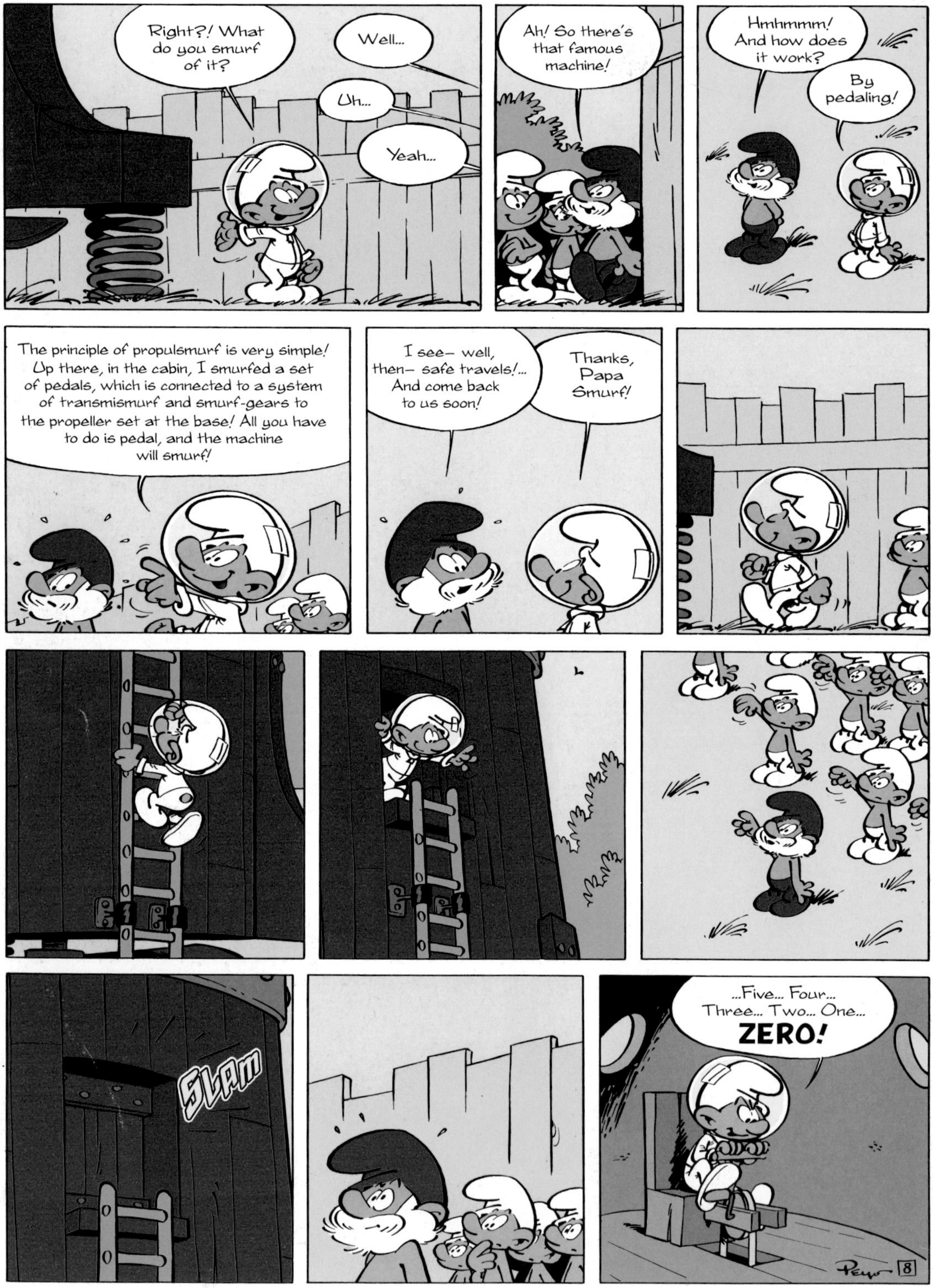
Right?! What do you smurf of it?
Well...
Uh...
Yeah...
Ah! So there's that famous machine!
Hmhmmm! And how does it work?
By pedaling!
The principle of propulsmurf is very simple! Up there, in the cabin, I smurfed a set of pedals, which is connected to a system of transmismurf and smurf-gears to the propeller set at the base! All you have to do is pedal, and the machine will smurf!
I see– well, then– safe travels!... And come back to us soon!
Thanks, Papa Smurf!
SLAM
...Five... Four... Three... Two... One... ZERO!
Peyo
8

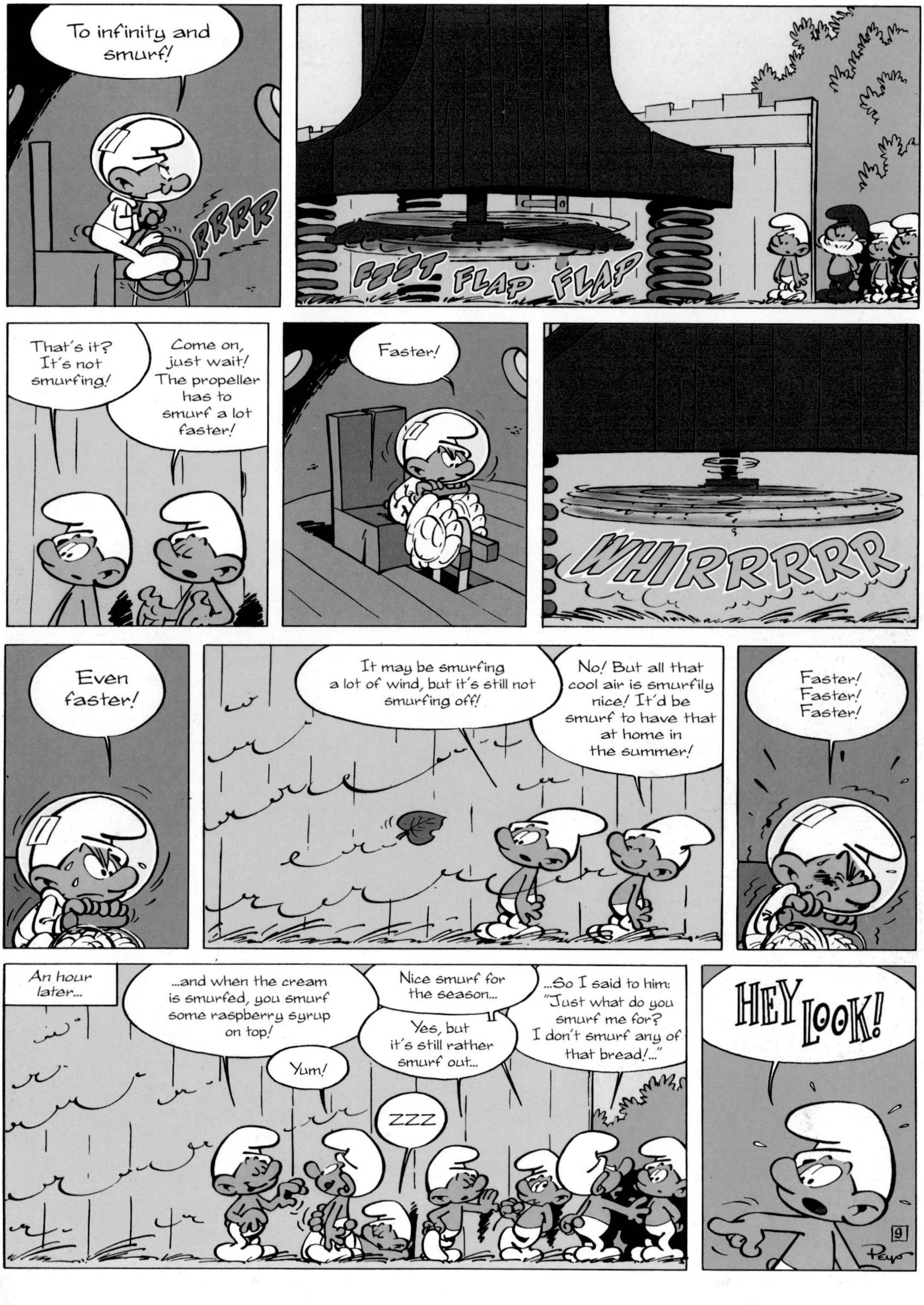

To infinity and smurf!
RRRR
FZZT FLAP FLAP
That's it? It's not smurfing!
Come on, just wait! The propeller has to smurf a lot faster!
Faster!
WHIRRRRR
Even faster!
It may be smurfing a lot of wind, but it's still not smurfing off!
No! But all that cool air is smurfily nice! It'd be smurf to have that at home in the summer!
Faster! Faster! Faster!
An hour later...
...and when the cream is smurfed, you smurf some raspberry syrup on top!
Yum!
Nice smurf for the season...
Yes, but it's still rather smurf out...
ZZZ
...So I said to him: "Just what do you smurf me for? I don't smurf any of that bread!..."
HEY LOOK!
9

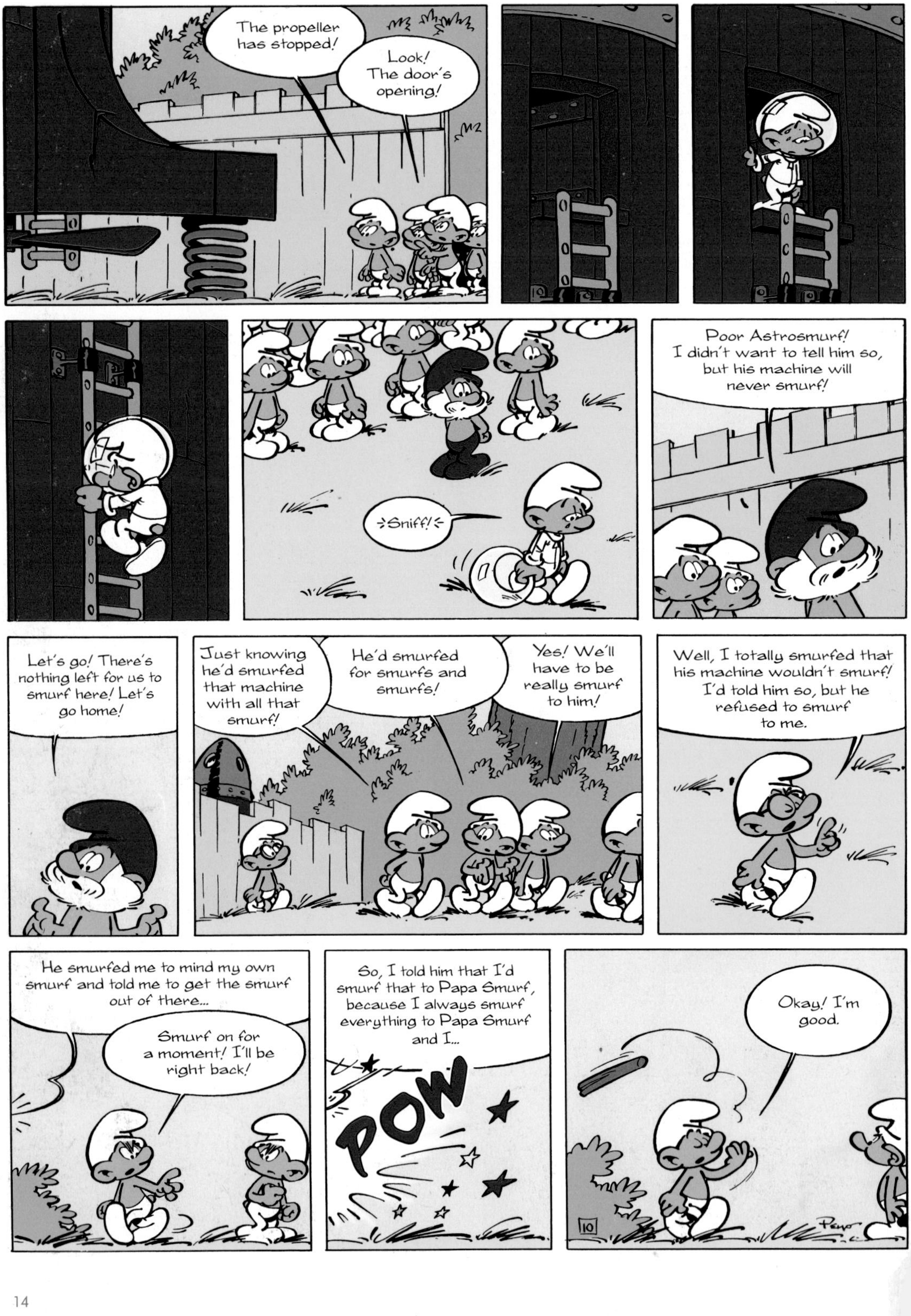

The propeller has stopped!
Look! The door's opening!
¬Sniff!¬
Poor Astrosmurf! I didn't want to tell him so, but his machine will never smurf!
Let's go! There's nothing left for us to smurf here! Let's go home!
Just knowing he'd smurfed that machine with all that smurf!
He'd smurfed for smurfs and smurfs!
Yes! We'll have to be really smurf to him!
Well, I totally smurfed that his machine wouldn't smurf! I'd told him so, but he refused to smurf to me.
He smurfed me to mind my own smurf and told me to get the smurf out of there...
Smurf on for a moment! I'll be right back!
So, I told him that I'd smurf that to Papa Smurf, because I always smurf everything to Papa Smurf and I...
POW
Okay! I'm good.
10
Peyo

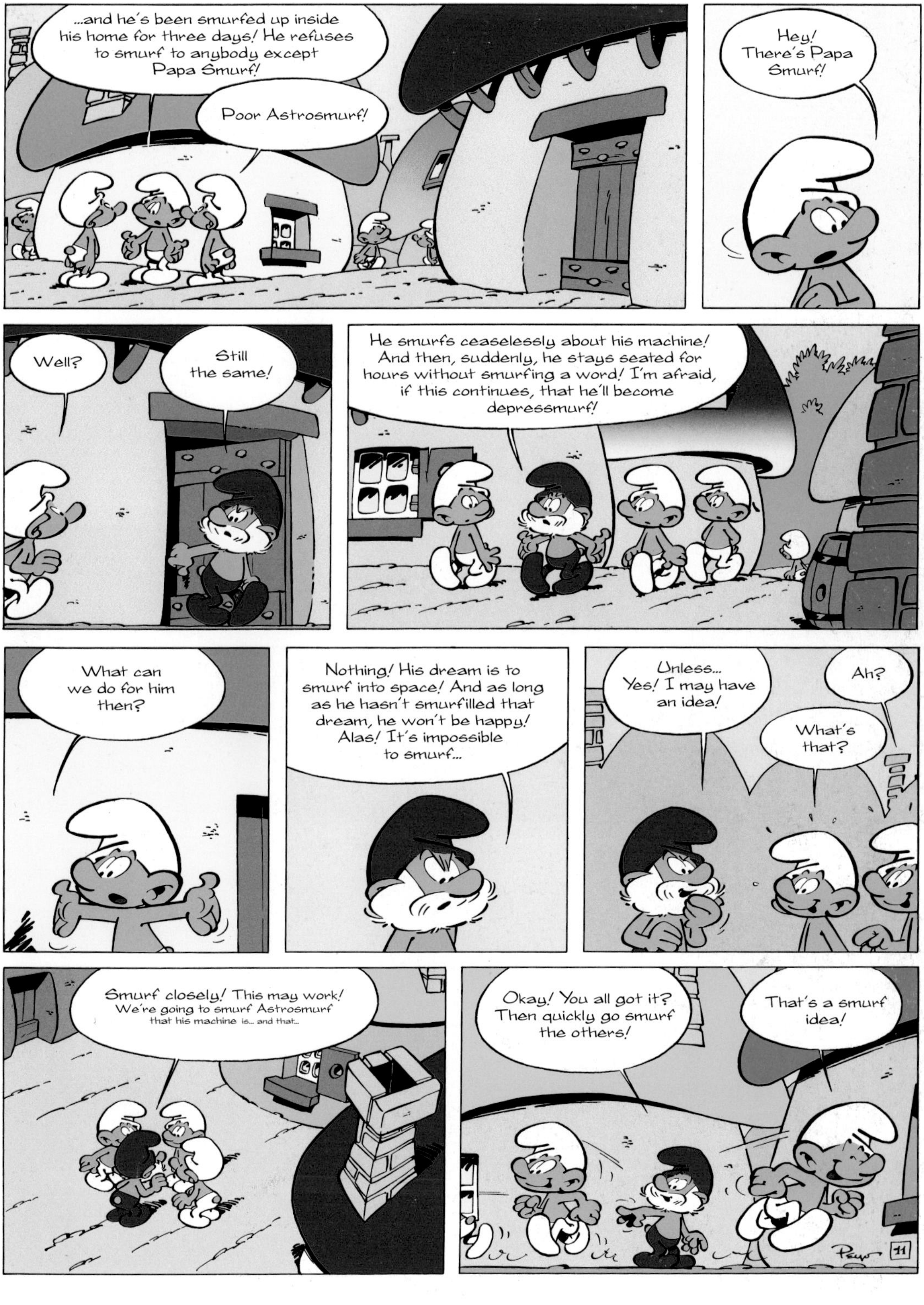
...and he's been smurfed up inside his home for three days! He refuses to smurf to anybody except Papa Smurf!
Poor Astrosmurf!
Hey! There's Papa Smurf!
Well?
Still the same!
He smurfs ceaselessly about his machine! And then, suddenly, he stays seated for hours without smurfing a word! I'm afraid, if this continues, that he'll become depressmurf!
What can we do for him then?
Nothing! His dream is to smurf into space! And as long as he hasn't smurfilled that dream, he won't be happy! Alas! It's impossible to smurf...
Unless... Yes! I may have an idea!
Ah?
What's that?
Smurf closely! This may work! We're going to smurf Astrosmurf that his machine is... and that...
Okay! You all got it? Then quickly go smurf the others!
That's a smurf idea!

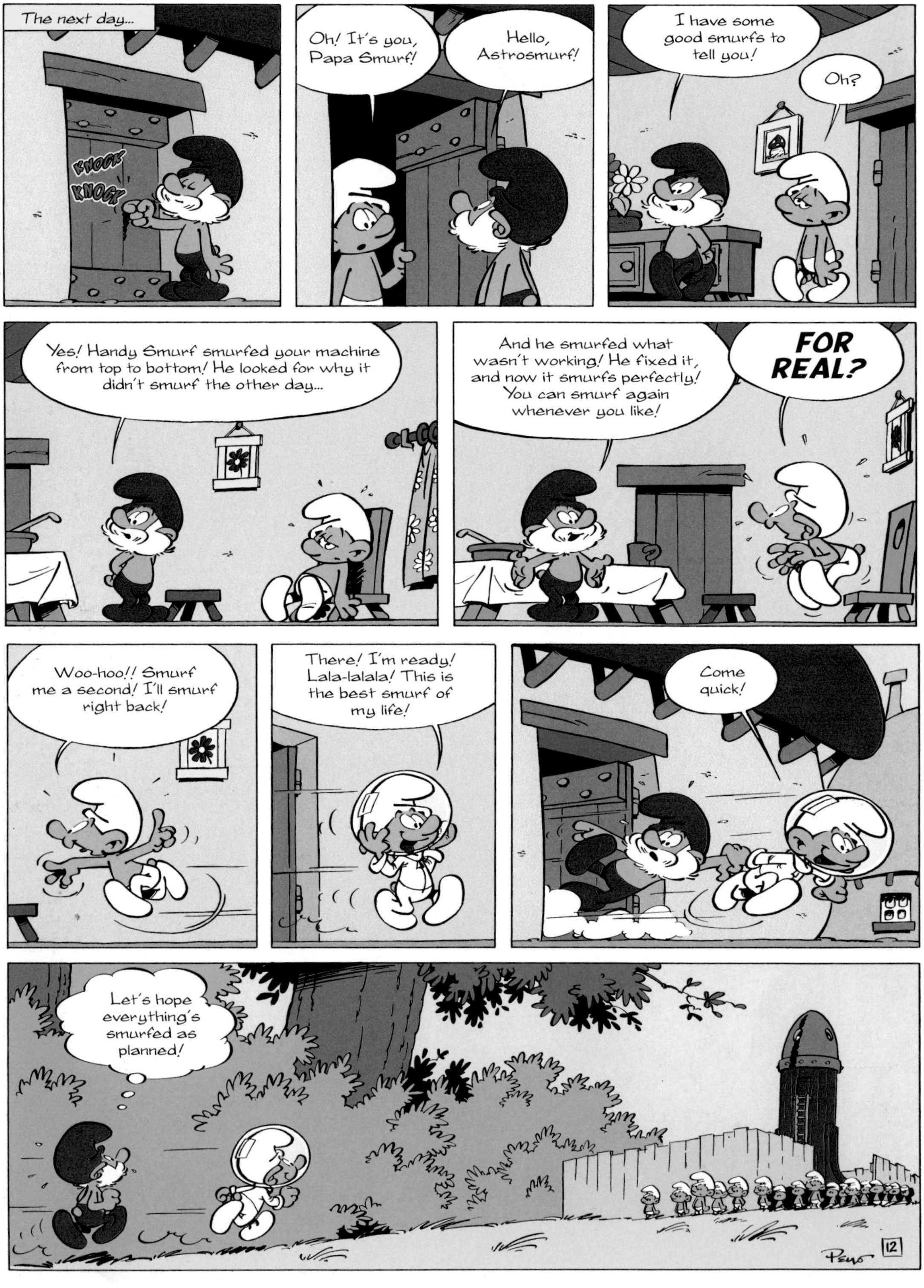
The next day...
KNOCK
KNOCK
Oh! It's you, Papa Smurf!
Hello, Astrosmurf!
I have some good smurfs to tell you!
Oh?
Yes! Handy Smurf smurfed your machine from top to bottom! He looked for why it didn't smurf the other day...
And he smurfed what wasn't working! He fixed it, and now it smurfs perfectly! You can smurf again whenever you like!
FOR REAL?
Woo-hoo!! Smurf me a second! I'll smurf right back!
There! I'm ready! Lala-lalala! This is the best smurf of my life!
Come quick!
Let's hope everything's smurfed as planned!
Peyo
12

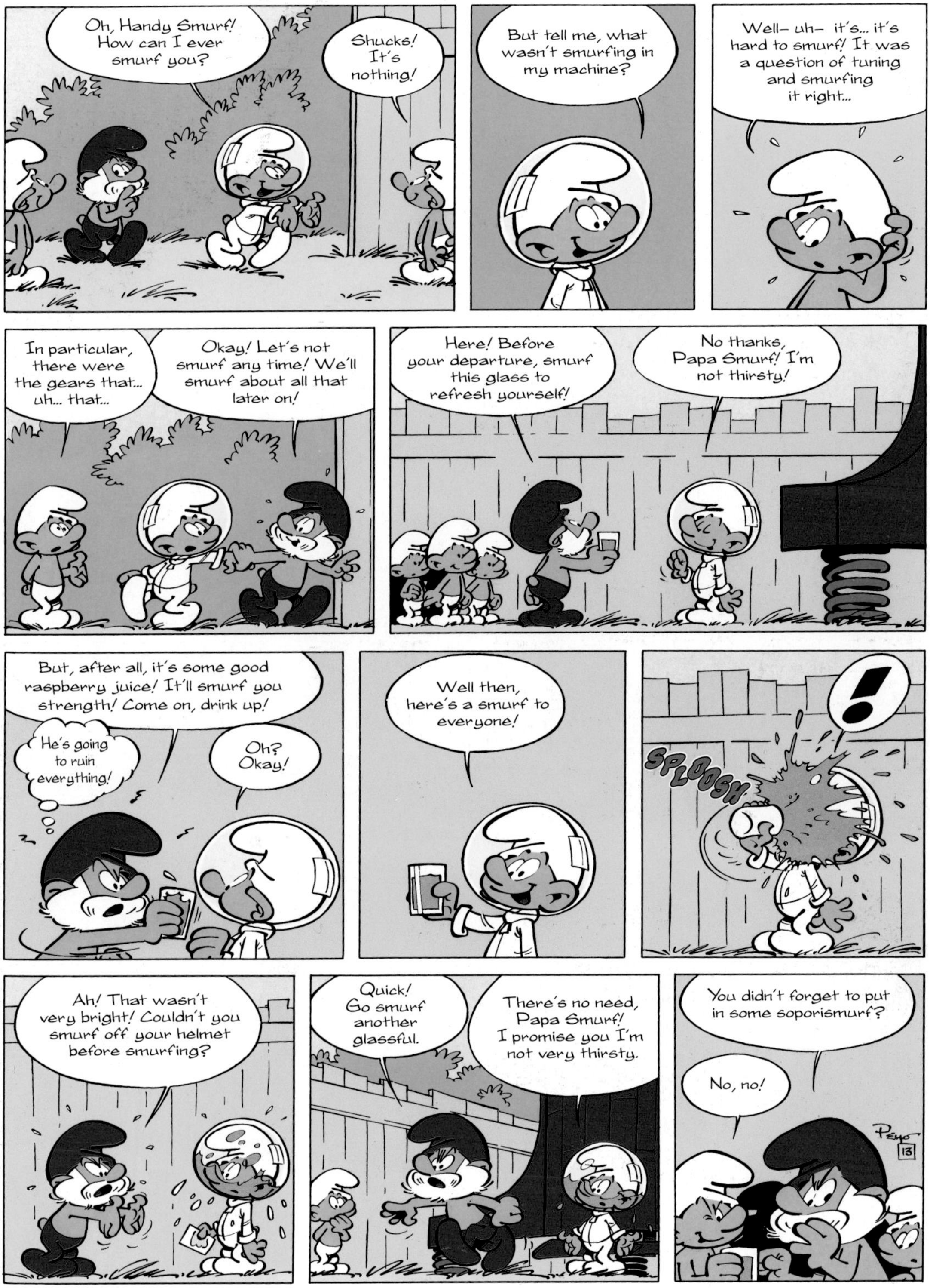

Oh, Handy Smurf! How can I ever smurf you?
Shucks! It's nothing!
But tell me, what wasn't smurfing in my machine?
Well- uh- it's... it's hard to smurf! It was a question of tuning and smurfing it right...
In particular, there were the gears that... uh... that...
Okay! Let's not smurf any time! We'll smurf about all that later on!
Here! Before your departure, smurf this glass to refresh yourself!
No thanks, Papa Smurf! I'm not thirsty!
But, after all, it's some good raspberry juice! It'll smurf you strength! Come on, drink up!
He's going to ruin everything!
Oh? Okay!
Well then, here's a smurf to everyone!
!
SPLOOSH
Ah! That wasn't very bright! Couldn't you smurf off your helmet before smurfing?
Quick! Go smurf another glassful.
There's no need, Papa Smurf! I promise you I'm not very thirsty.
You didn't forget to put in some soporismurf?
No, no!

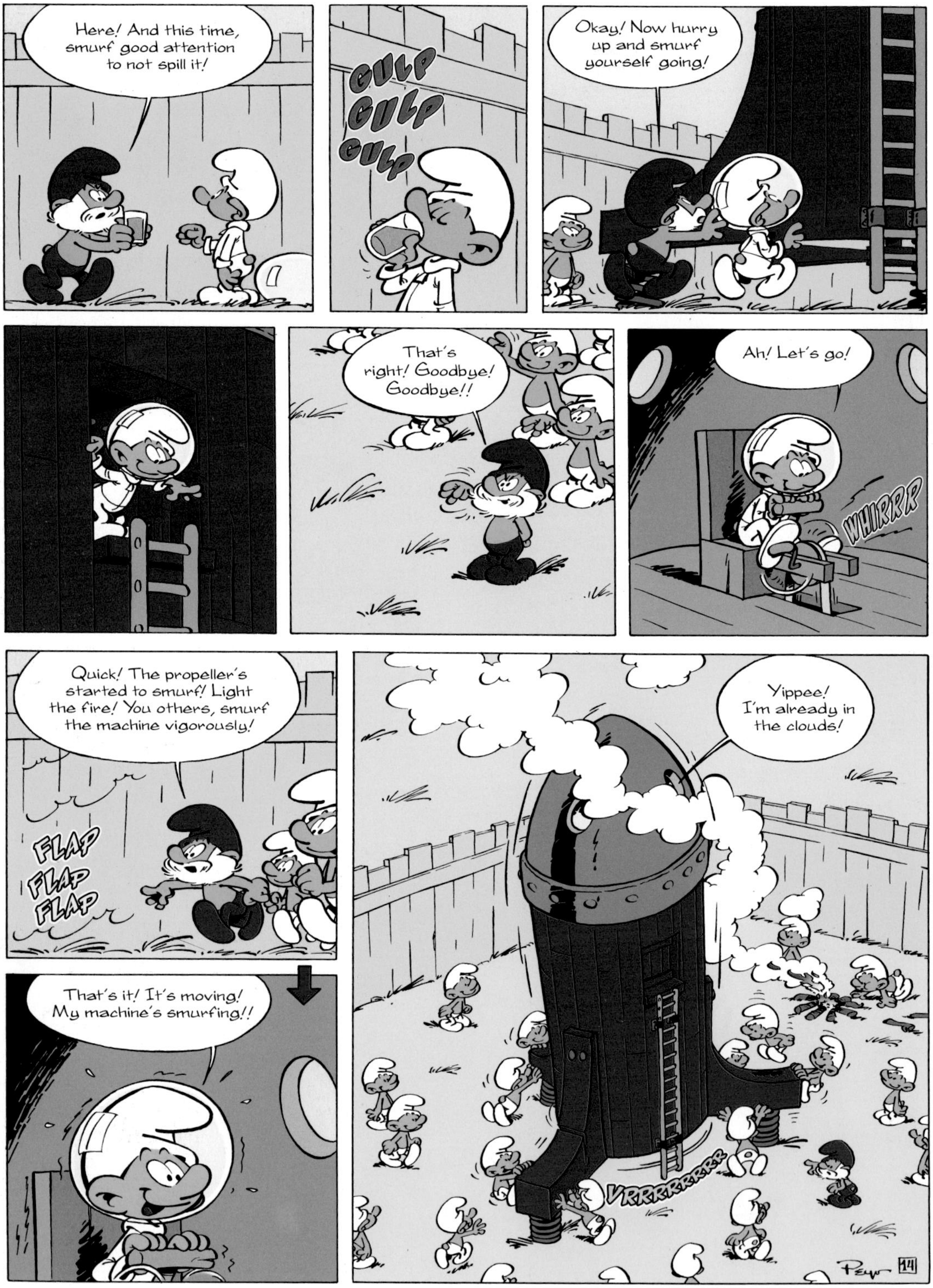
Here! And this time, smurf good attention to not spill it!
GULP GULP GULP
Okay! Now hurry up and smurf yourself going!
That's right! Goodbye! Goodbye!!
Ah! Let's go!
WHIRRR
Quick! The propeller's started to smurf! Light the fire! You others, smurf the machine vigorously!
FLAP FLAP FLAP
That's it! It's moving! My machine's smurfing!!
Yippee! I'm already in the clouds!
VRRRRRRRR
Peyo
14

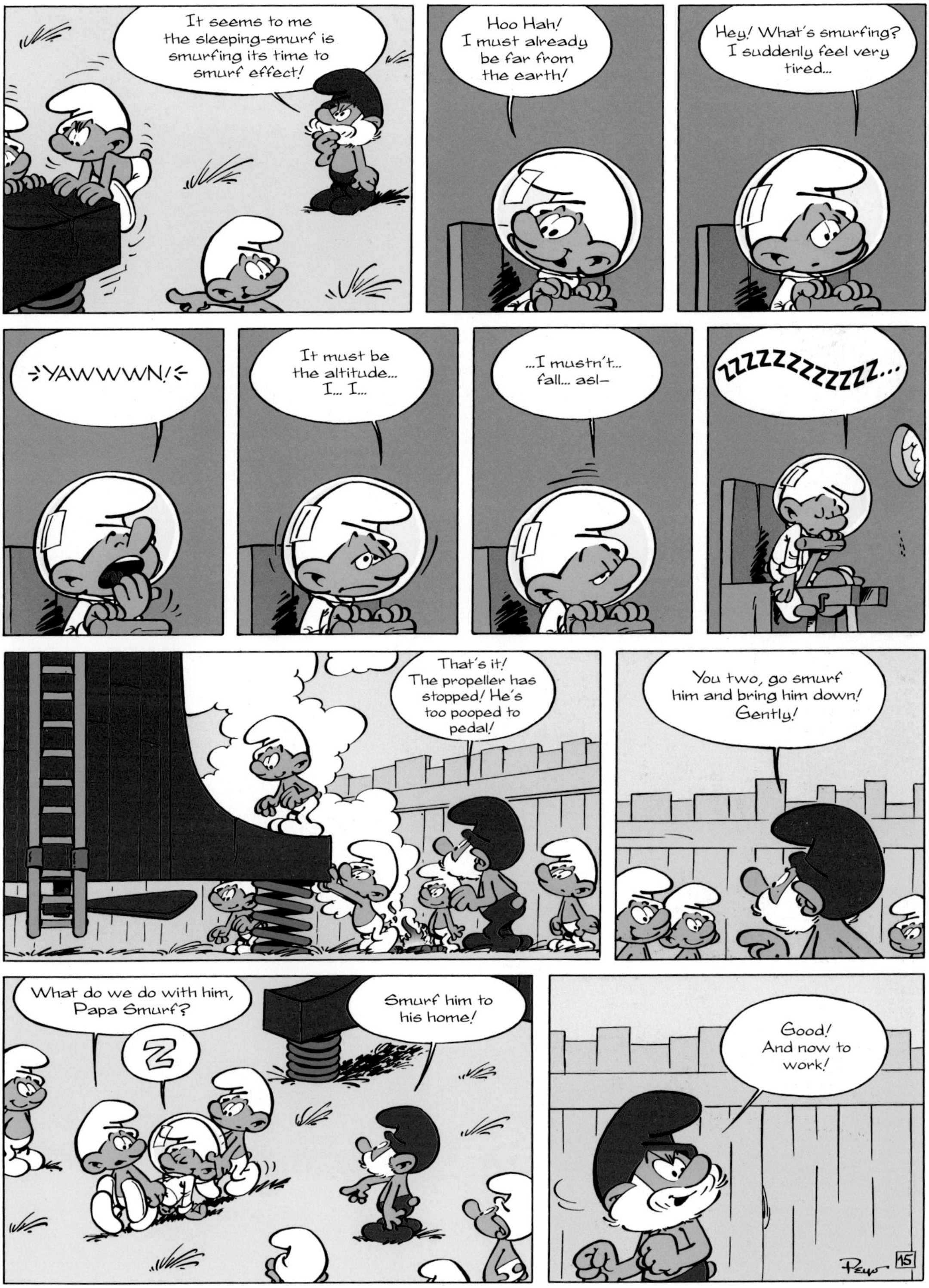

It seems to me the sleeping-smurf is smurfing its time to smurf effect!
Hoo Hah! I must already be far from the earth!
Hey! What's smurfing? I suddenly feel very tired...
YAWWWN!
It must be the altitude... I... I...
...I mustn't... fall... asl–
ZZZZZZZZZZZ...
That's it! The propeller has stopped! He's too pooped to pedal!
You two, go smurf him and bring him down! Gently!
What do we do with him, Papa Smurf?
Z
Smurf him to his home!
Good! And now to work!
15

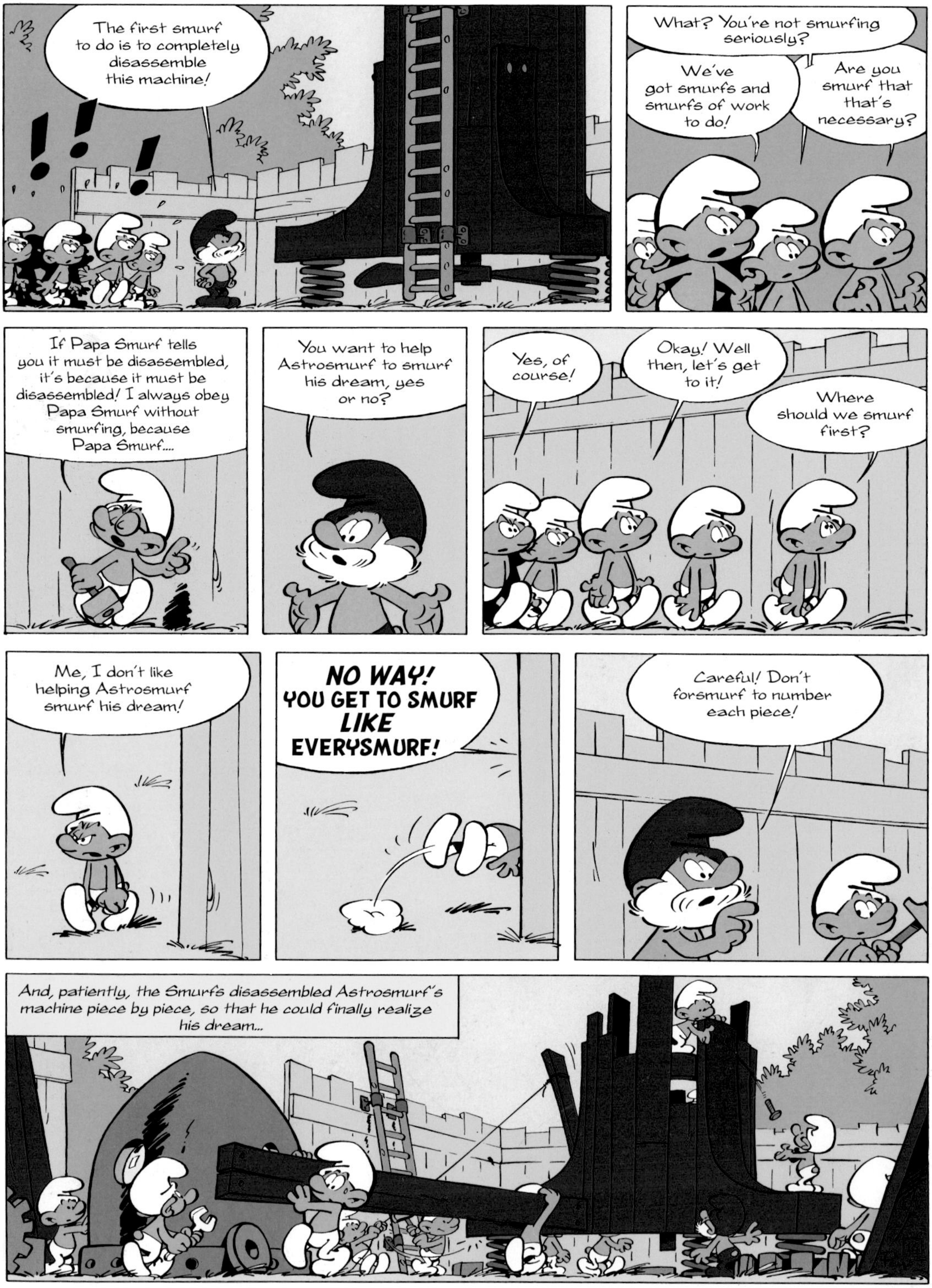
The first smurf to do is to completely disassemble this machine!
! ! !
What? You're not smurfing seriously?
We've got smurfs and smurfs of work to do!
Are you smurf that that's necessary?
If Papa Smurf tells you it must be disassembled, it's because it must be disassembled! I always obey Papa Smurf without smurfing, because Papa Smurf....
You want to help Astrosmurf to smurf his dream, yes or no?
Yes, of course!
Okay! Well then, let's get to it!
Where should we smurf first?
Me, I don't like helping Astrosmurf smurf his dream!
NO WAY! YOU GET TO SMURF LIKE EVERYSMURF!
Careful! Don't forsmurf to number each piece!
And, patiently, the Smurfs disassembled Astrosmurf's machine piece by piece, so that he could finally realize his dream...

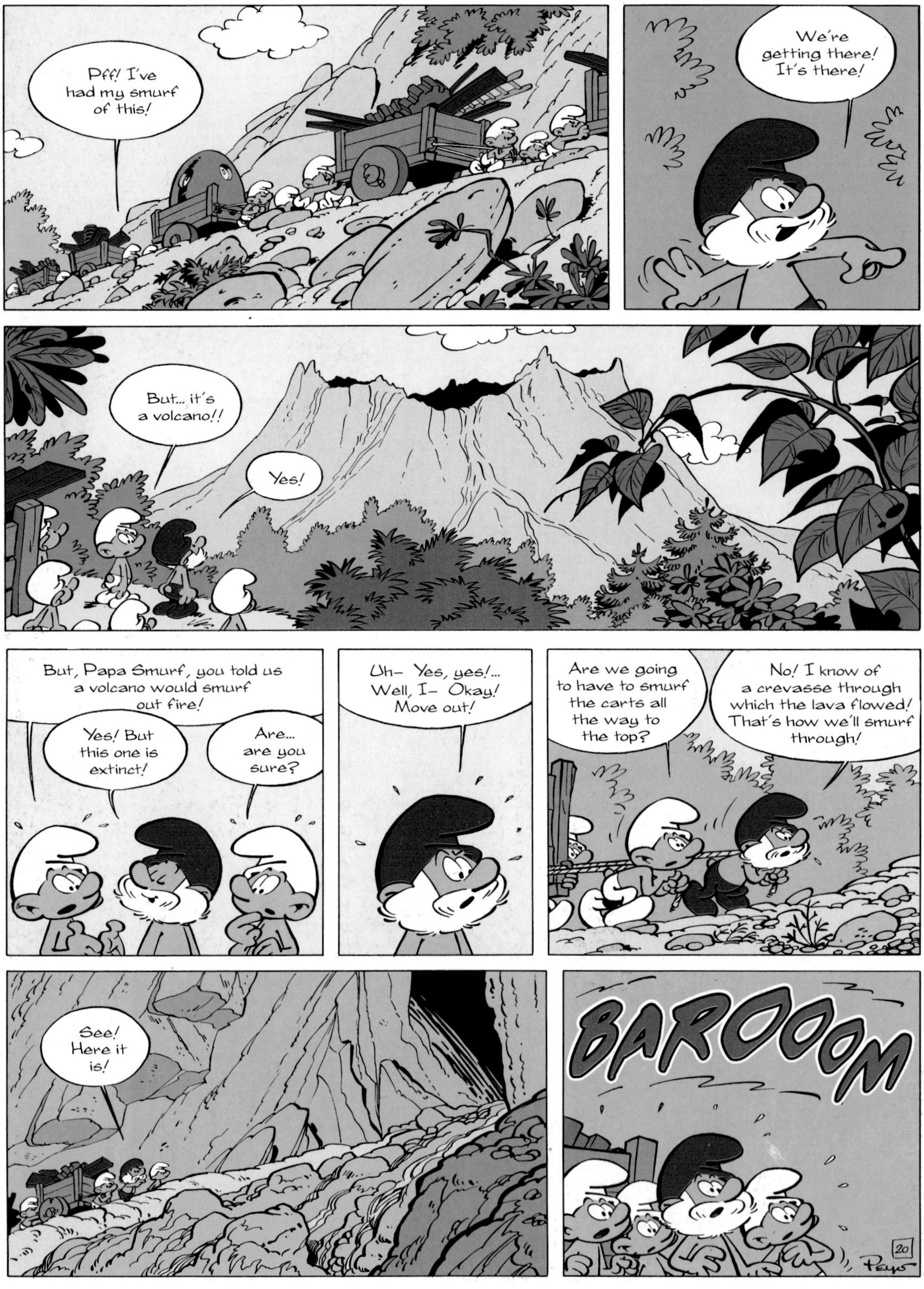
Pff! I've had my smurf of this!
We're getting there! It's there!
But... it's a volcano!!
Yes!
But, Papa Smurf, you told us a volcano would smurf out fire!
Yes! But this one is extinct!
Are... are you sure?
Uh- Yes, yes!... Well, I- Okay! Move out!
Are we going to have to smurf the carts all the way to the top?
No! I know of a crevasse through which the lava flowed! That's how we'll smurf through!
See! Here it is!
BAROOOM
20
Peyo

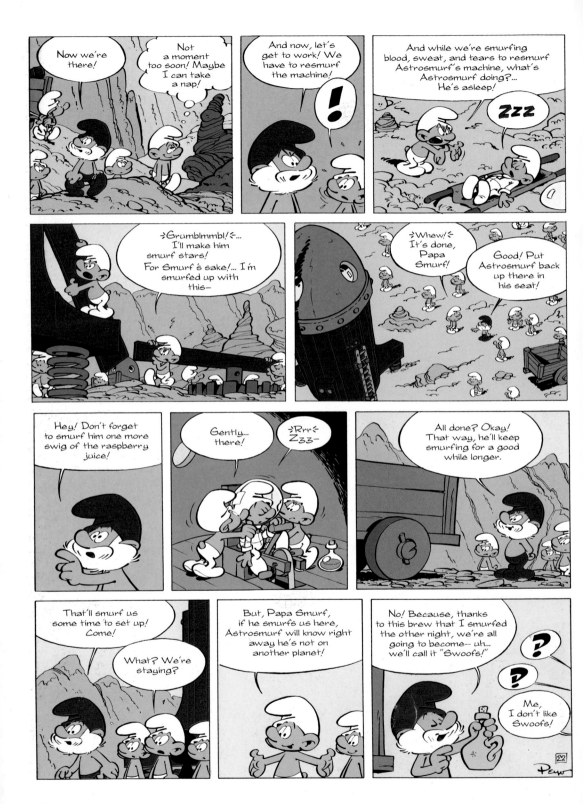

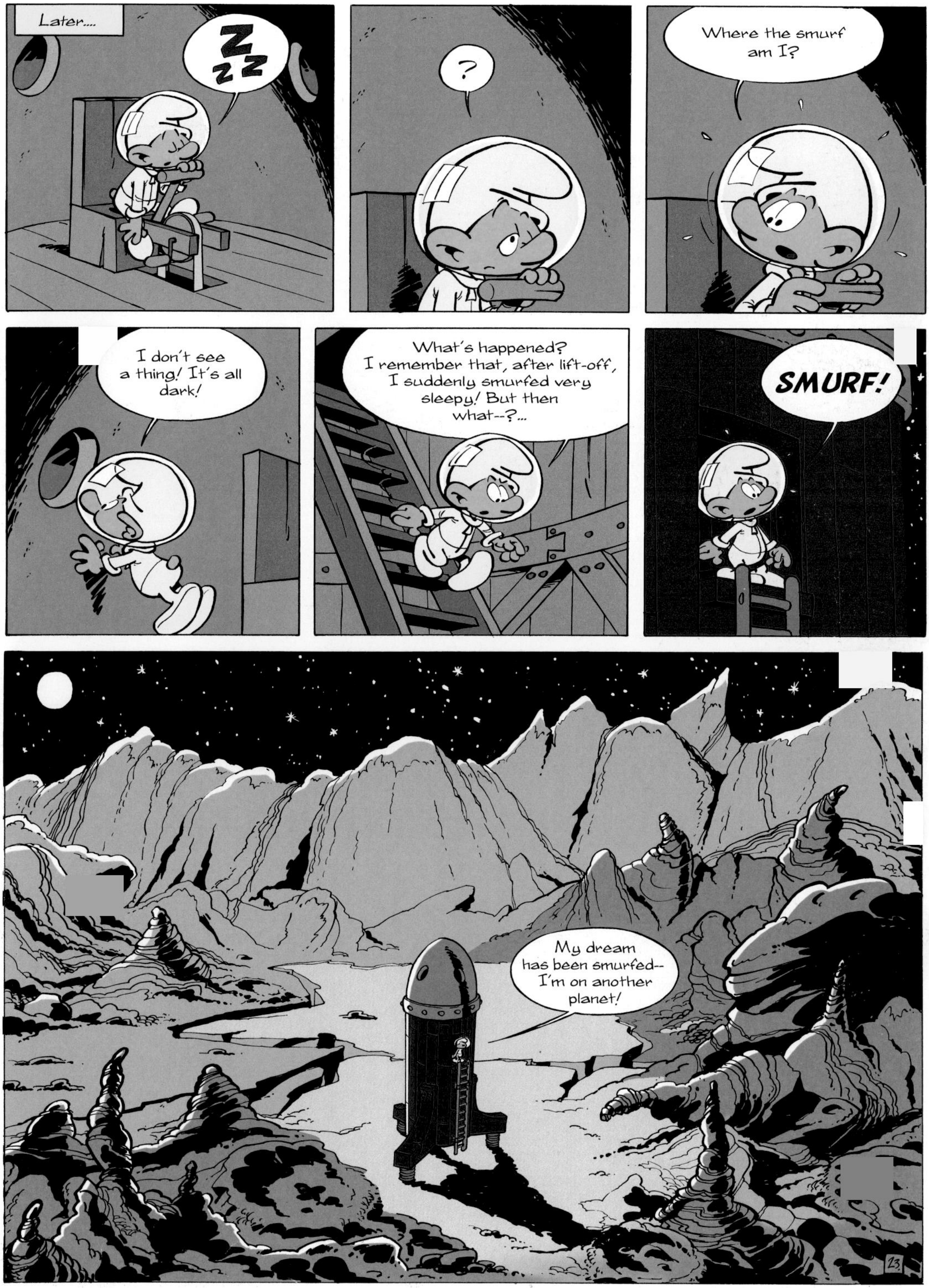

Later....
ZZZ
?
Where the smurf am I?
I don't see a thing! It's all dark!
What's happened? I remember that, after lift-off, I suddenly smurfed very sleepy! But then what--?...
SMURF!
My dream has been smurfed-- I'm on another planet!

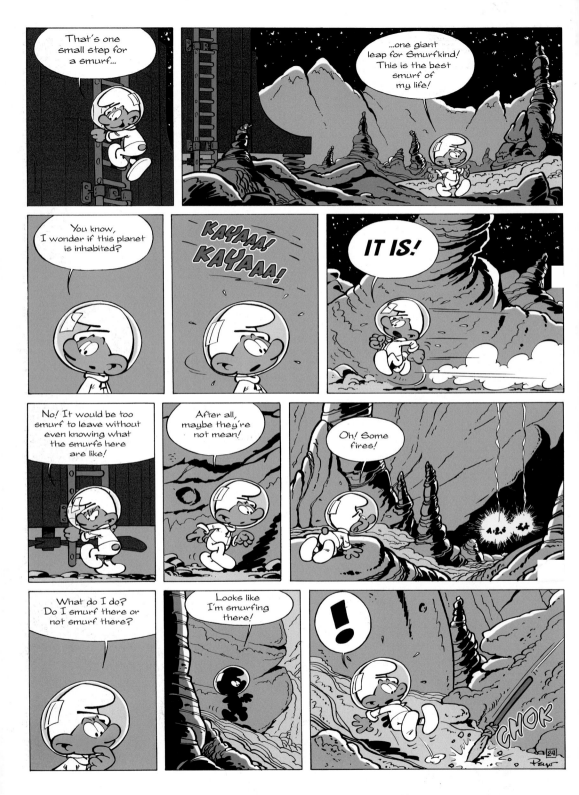

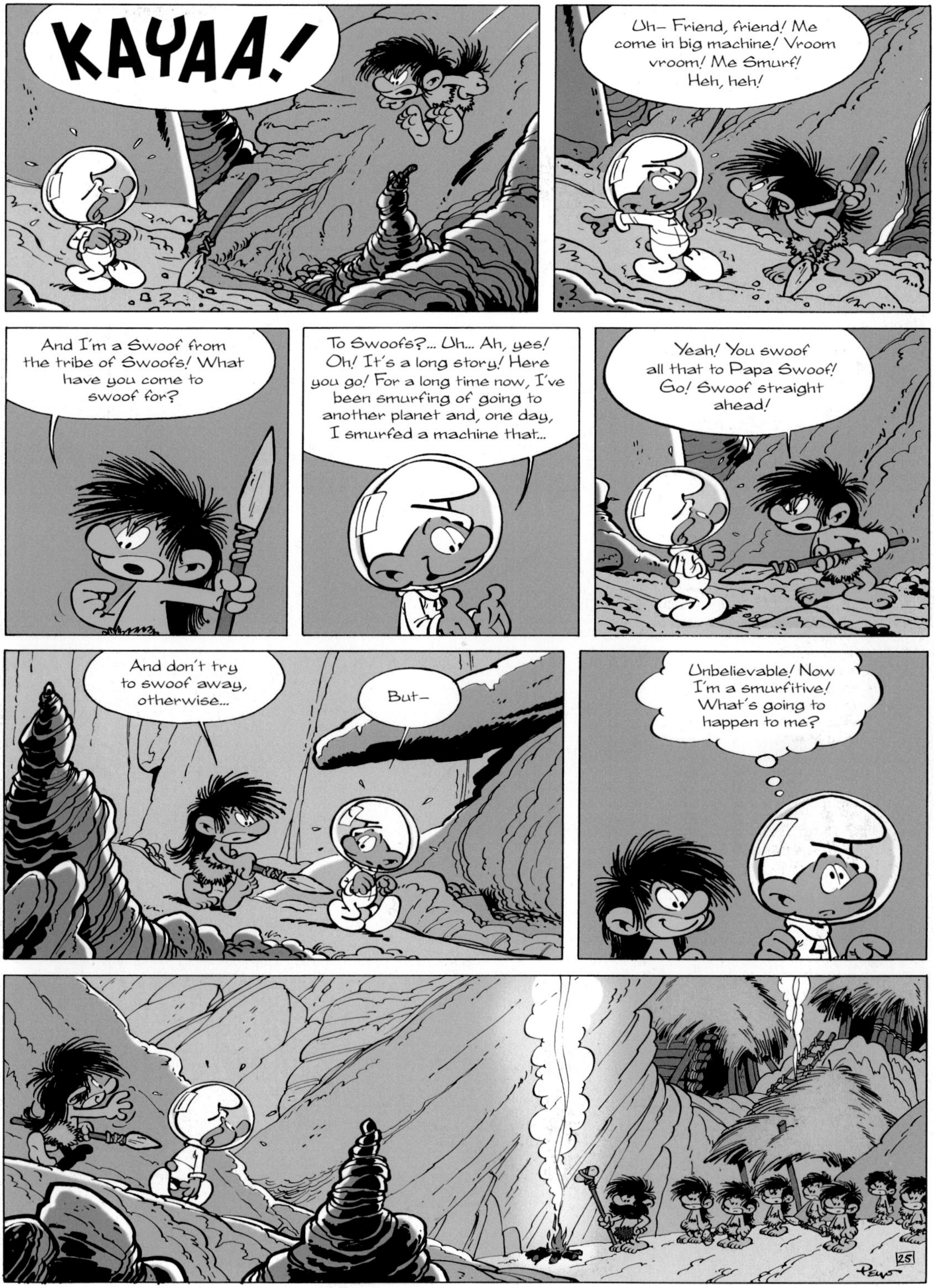
KAYAA!
Uh– Friend, friend! Me come in big machine! Vroom vroom! Me Smurf! Heh, heh!
And I'm a Swoof from the tribe of Swoofs! What have you come to swoof for?
To Swoofs?... Uh... Ah, yes! Oh! It's a long story! Here you go! For a long time now, I've been smurfing of going to another planet and, one day, I smurfed a machine that...
Yeah! You swoof all that to Papa Swoof! Go! Swoof straight ahead!
And don't try to swoof away, otherwise...
But–
Unbelievable! Now I'm a smurfitive! What's going to happen to me?
25
PEYO

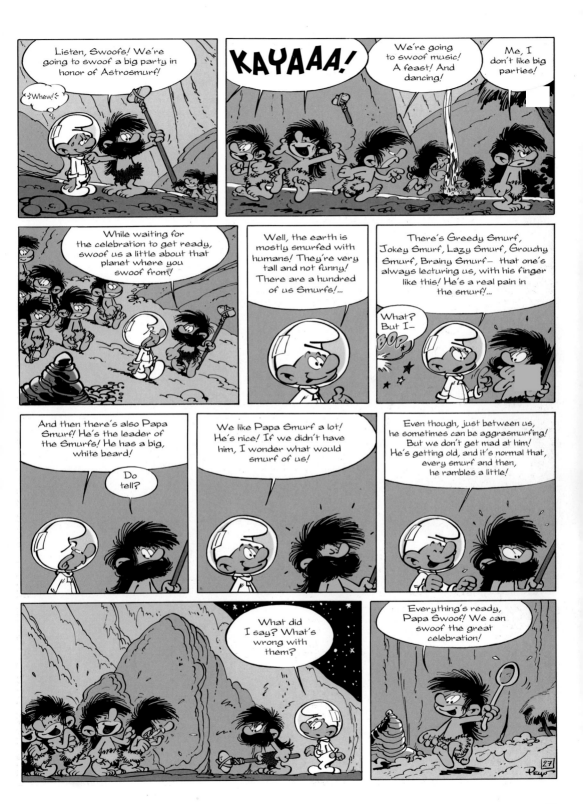

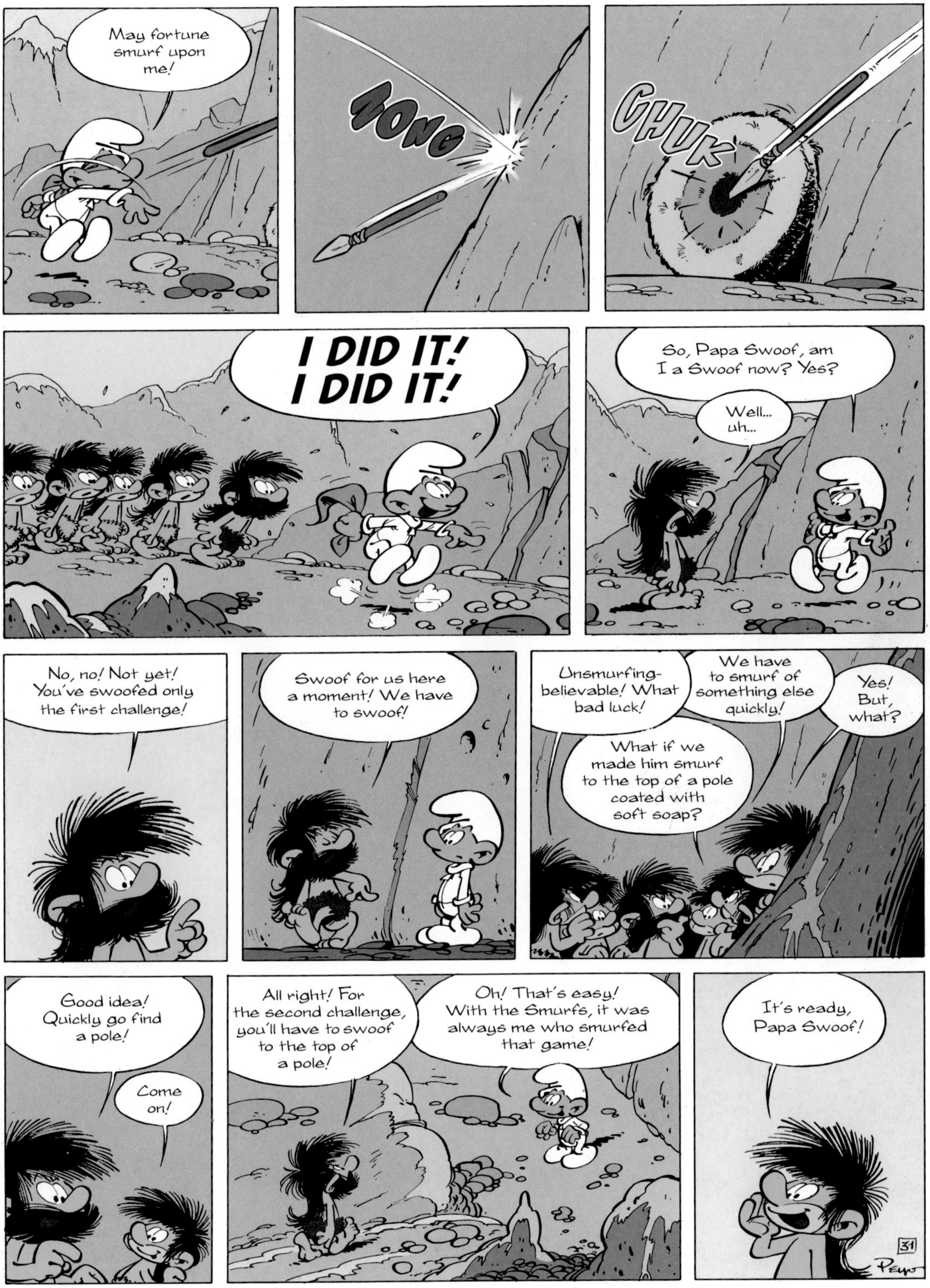
May fortune smurf upon me!
DONG
CHUK
I DID IT! I DID IT!
So, Papa Swoof, am I a Swoof now? Yes?
Well... uh...
No, no! Not yet! You've swoofed only the first challenge!
Swoof for us here a moment! We have to swoof!
Unsmurfing-believable! What bad luck!
We have to smurf of something else quickly!
Yes! But, what?
What if we made him smurf to the top of a pole coated with soft soap?
Good idea! Quickly go find a pole!
Come on!
All right! For the second challenge, you'll have to swoof to the top of a pole!
Oh! That's easy! With the Smurfs, it was always me who smurfed that game!
It's ready, Papa Swoof!
31
Peyo

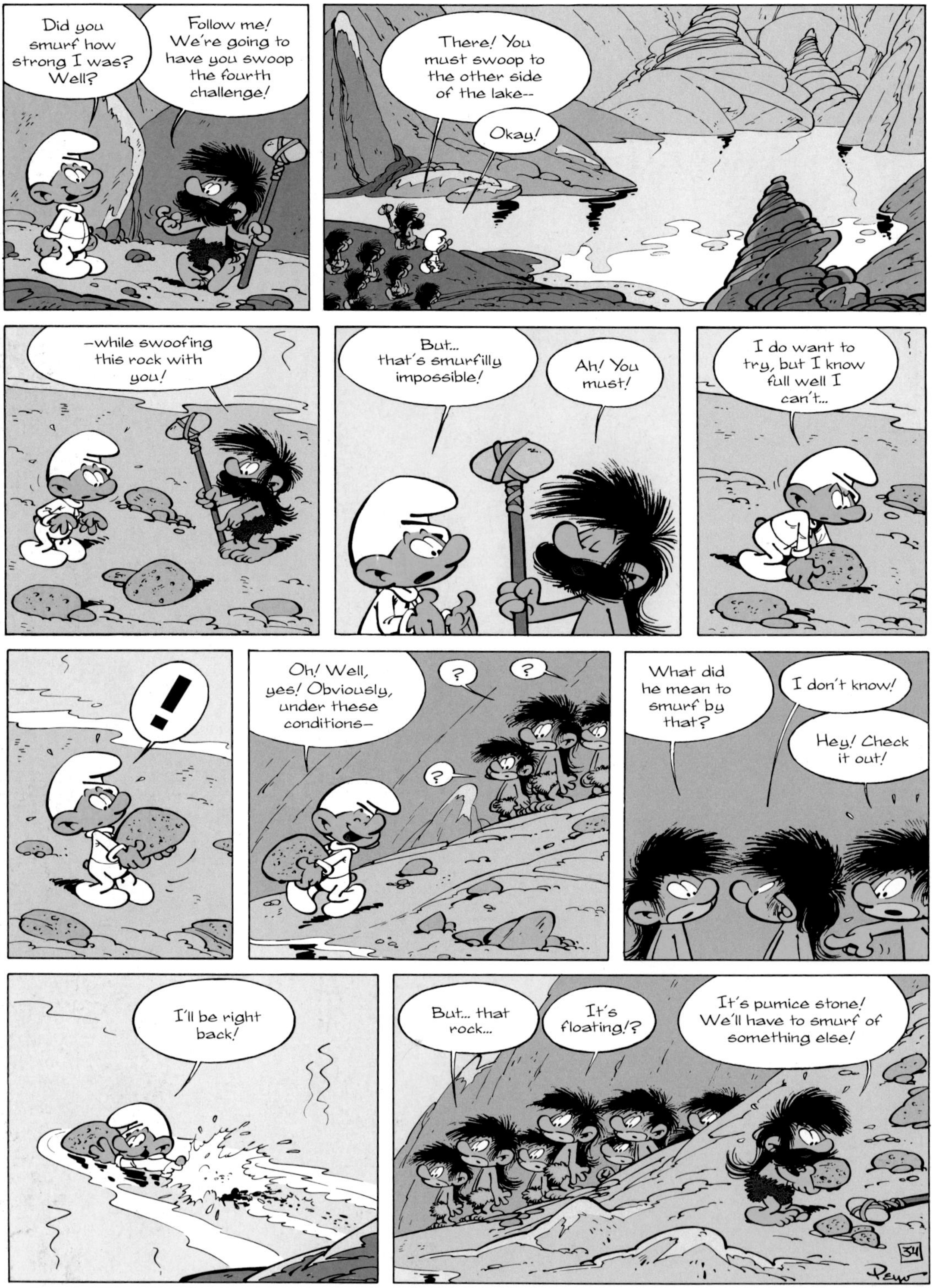
Did you smurf how strong I was? Well?
Follow me! We're going to have you swoop the fourth challenge!
There! You must swoop to the other side of the lake--
Okay!
-while swoofing this rock with you!
But... that's smurfilly impossible!
Ah! You must!
I do want to try, but I know full well I can't...
!
Oh! Well, yes! Obviously, under these conditions-
?
?
?
What did he mean to smurf by that?
I don't know!
Hey! Check it out!
I'll be right back!
But... that rock...
It's floating!?
It's pumice stone! We'll have to smurf of something else!
34
Peyo

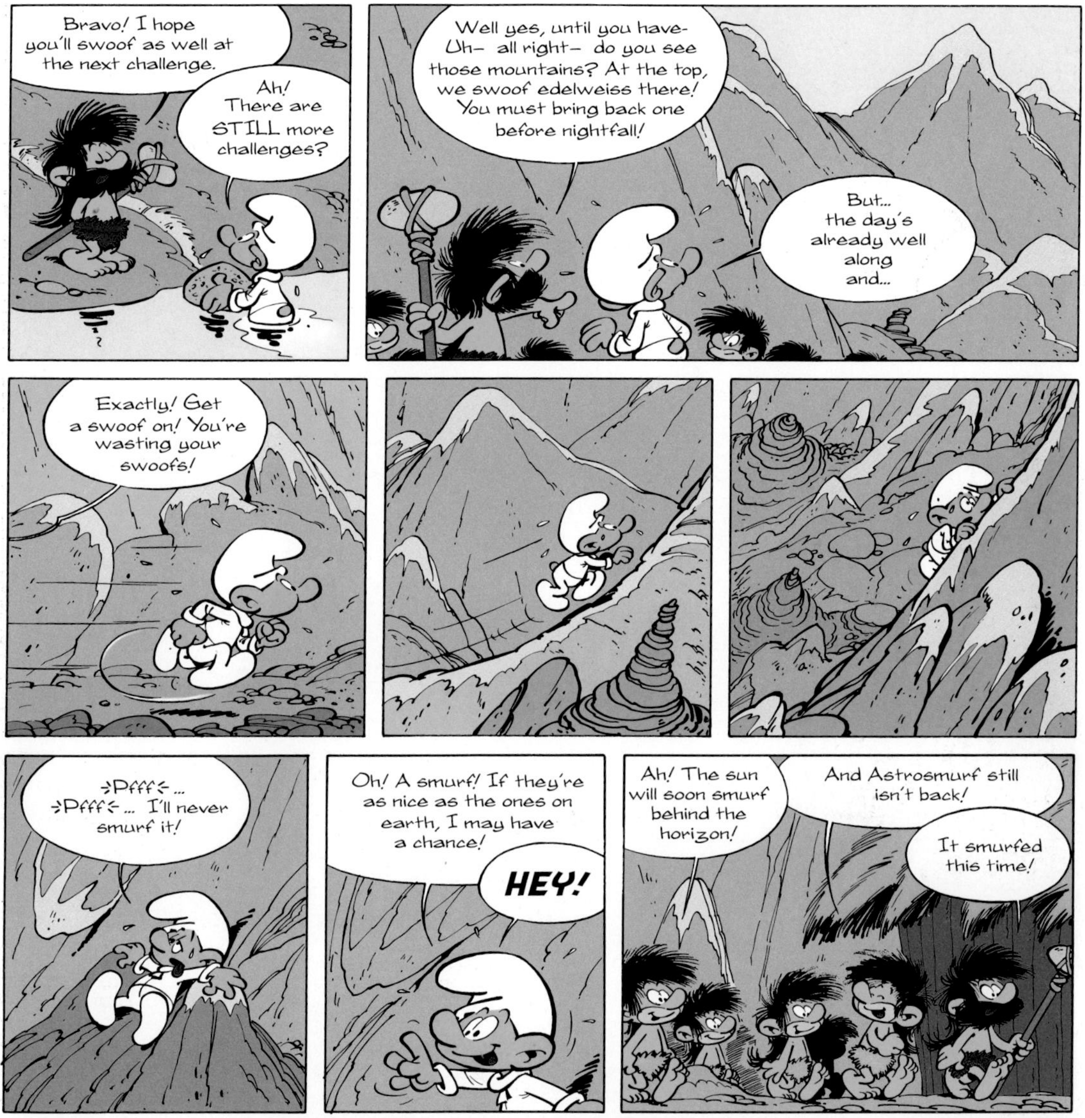

Bravo! I hope you'll swoof as well at the next challenge.
Ah! There are STILL more challenges?
Well yes, until you have- Uh- all right- do you see those mountains? At the top, we swoof edelweiss there! You must bring back one before nightfall!
But... the day's already well along and...
Exactly! Get a swoof on! You're wasting your swoofs!
⇉Pfff⇇... ⇉Pfff⇇... I'll never smurf it!
Oh! A smurf! If they're as nice as the ones on earth, I may have a chance!
HEY!
Ah! The sun will soon smurf behind the horizon!
And Astrosmurf still isn't back!
It smurfed this time!
Yoohoo! Here I am!
And here's an edelweiss!
35

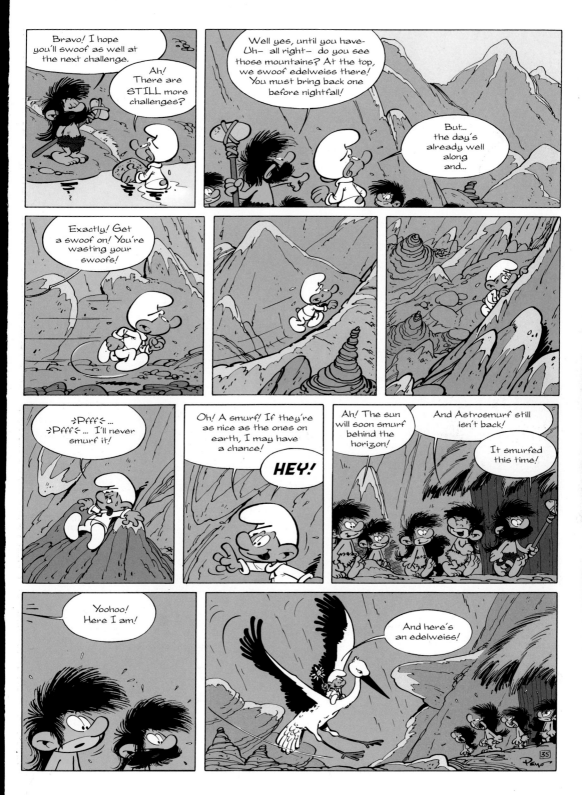

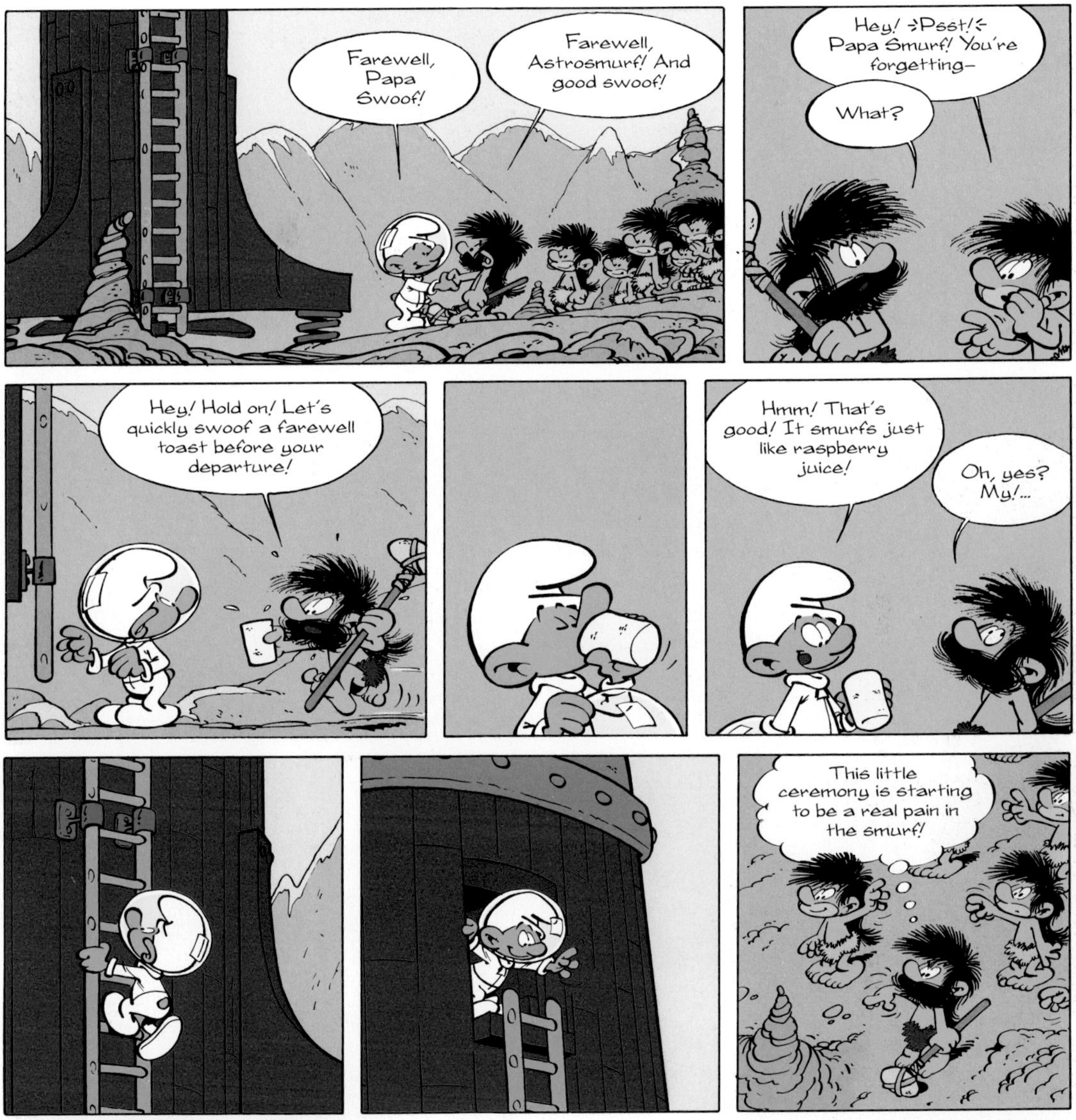
Farewell, Papa Swoof!
Farewell, Astrosmurf! And good swoof!
Hey! ⁑Psst!⁑ Papa Smurf! You're forgetting–
What?
Hey! Hold on! Let's quickly swoof a farewell toast before your departure!
Hmm! That's good! It smurfs just like raspberry juice!
Oh, yes? My!...
This little ceremony is starting to be a real pain in the smurf!
FLAP FLAP FLAP
⁑Rrrr⁑... Zzz...
⁑Whew!⁑ That's it!

43

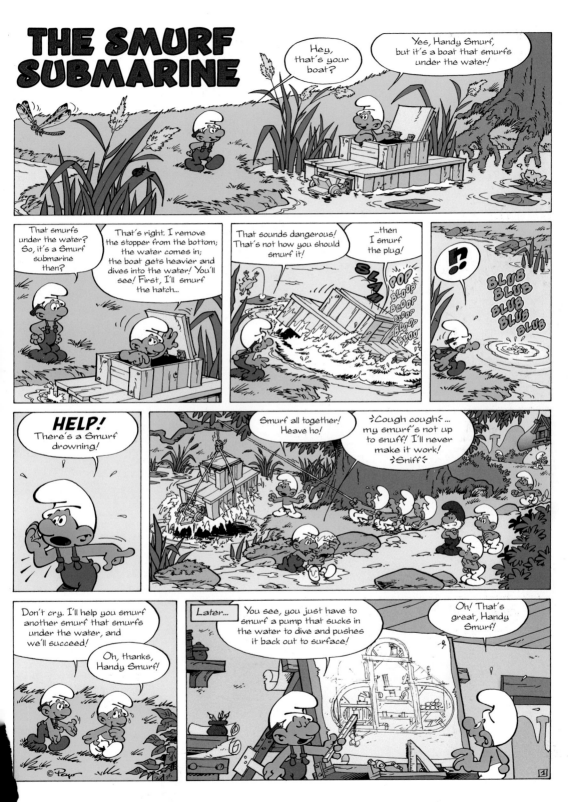

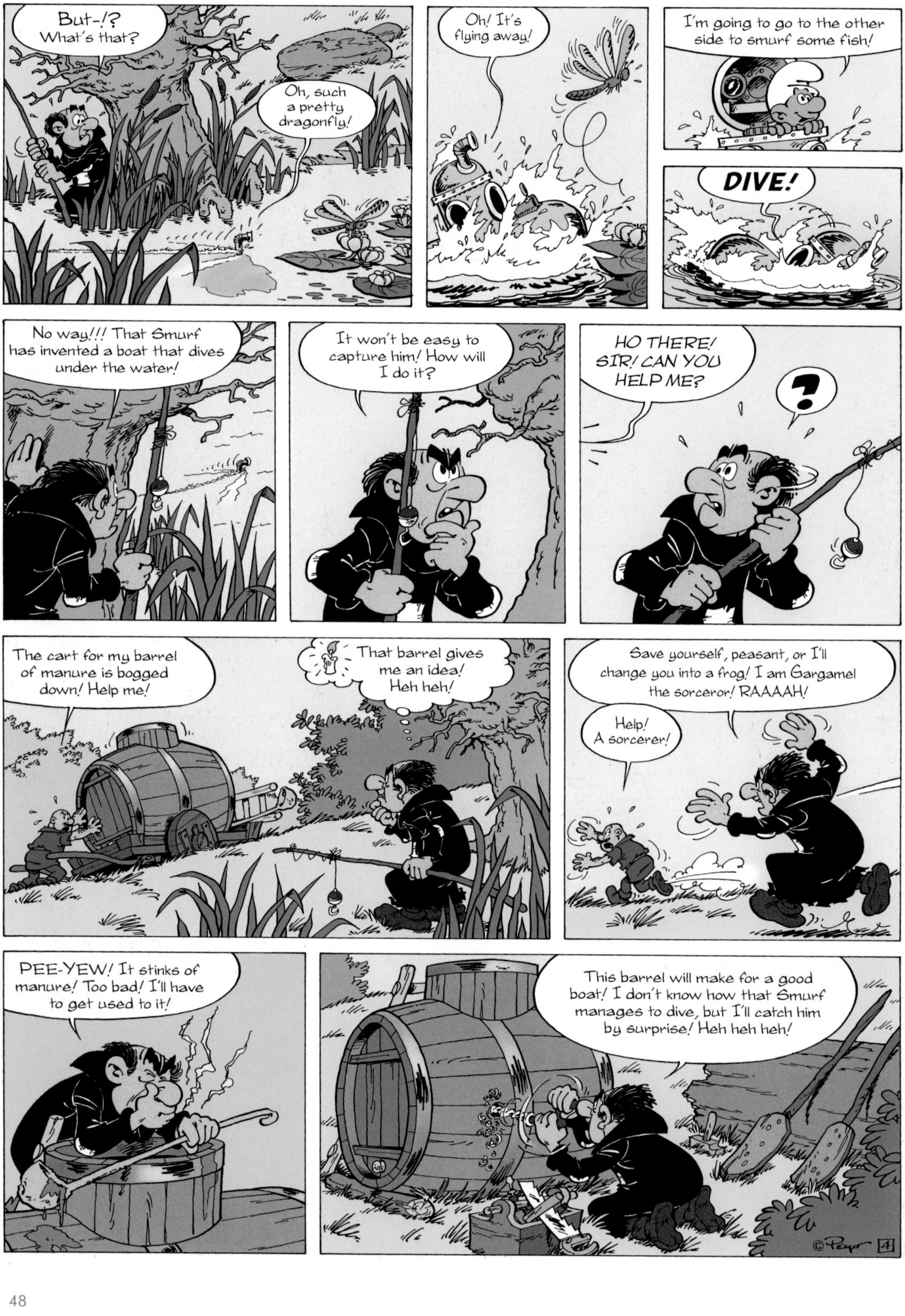
But-!? What's that?
Oh, such a pretty dragonfly!
Oh! It's flying away!
I'm going to go to the other side to smurf some fish!
DIVE!
No way!!! That Smurf has invented a boat that dives under the water!
It won't be easy to capture him! How will I do it?
HO THERE! SIR! CAN YOU HELP ME?
?
The cart for my barrel of manure is bogged down! Help me!
That barrel gives me an idea! Heh heh!
Save yourself, peasant, or I'll change you into a frog! I am Gargamel the sorceror! RAAAAH!
Help! A sorcerer!
PEE-YEW! It stinks of manure! Too bad! I'll have to get used to it!
This barrel will make for a good boat! I don't know how that Smurf manages to dive, but I'll catch him by surprise! Heh heh heh!
© Peyo 4

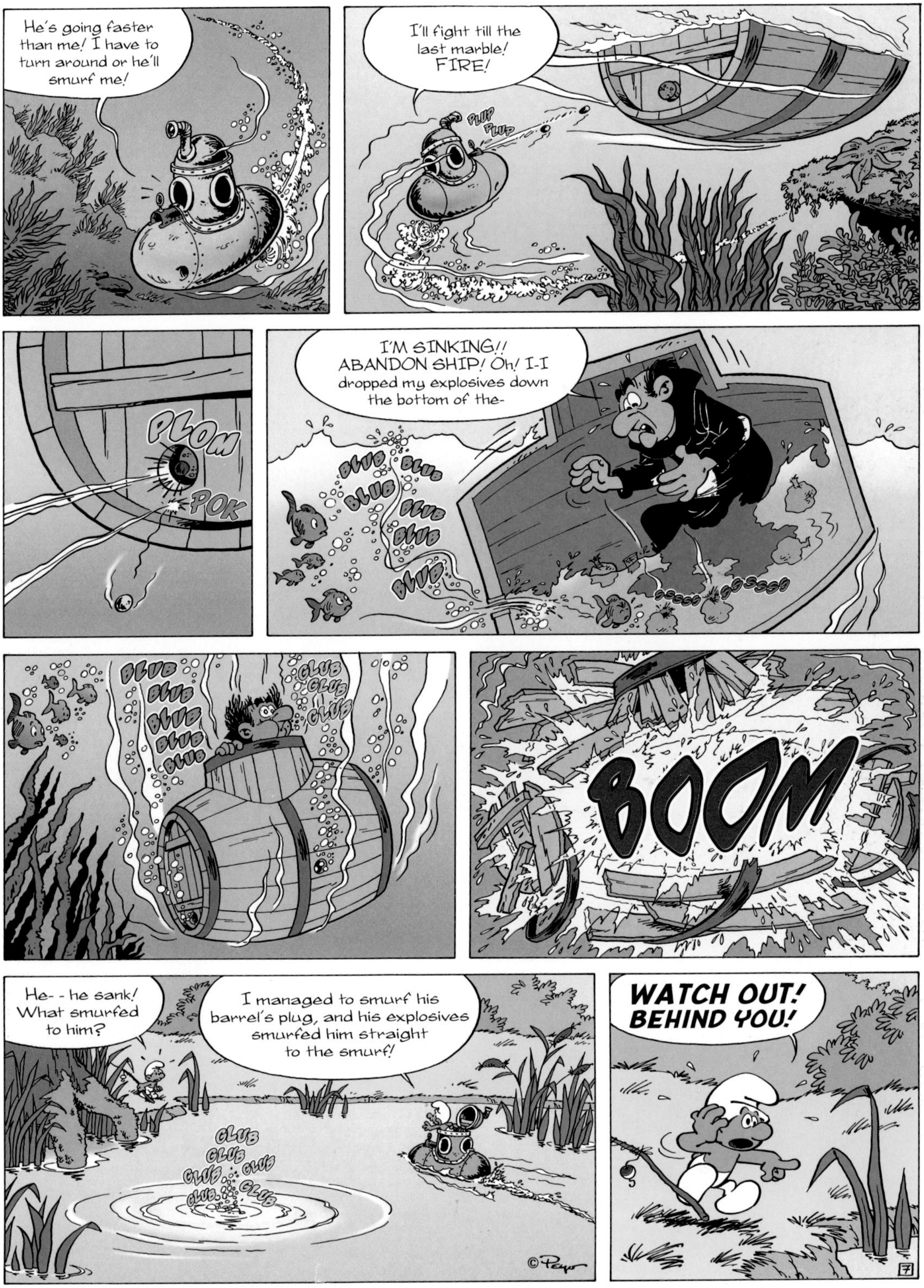
He's going faster than me! I have to turn around or he'll smurf me!
I'll fight till the last marble! FIRE!
PLUP PLUP
PLOM
POK
I'M SINKING!! ABANDON SHIP! Oh! I-I dropped my explosives down the bottom of the-
BLUB BLUB BLUB BLUB BLUB BLUB
BLUB BLUB BLUB BLUB BLUB
CLUB CLUB CLUB
BOOM
He- - he sank! What smurfed to him?
I managed to smurf his barrel's plug, and his explosives smurfed him straight to the smurf!
CLUB CLUB CLUB CLUB CLUB CLUB
© Peyo
WATCH OUT! BEHIND YOU!
7

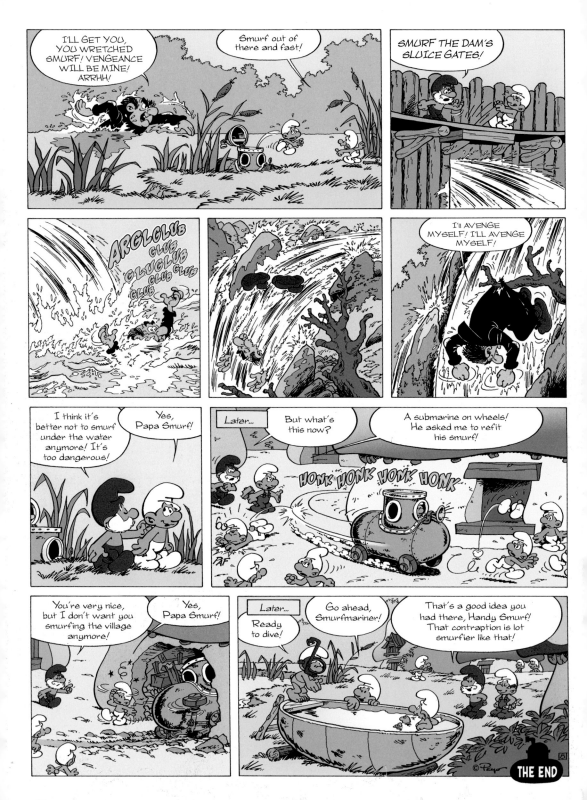

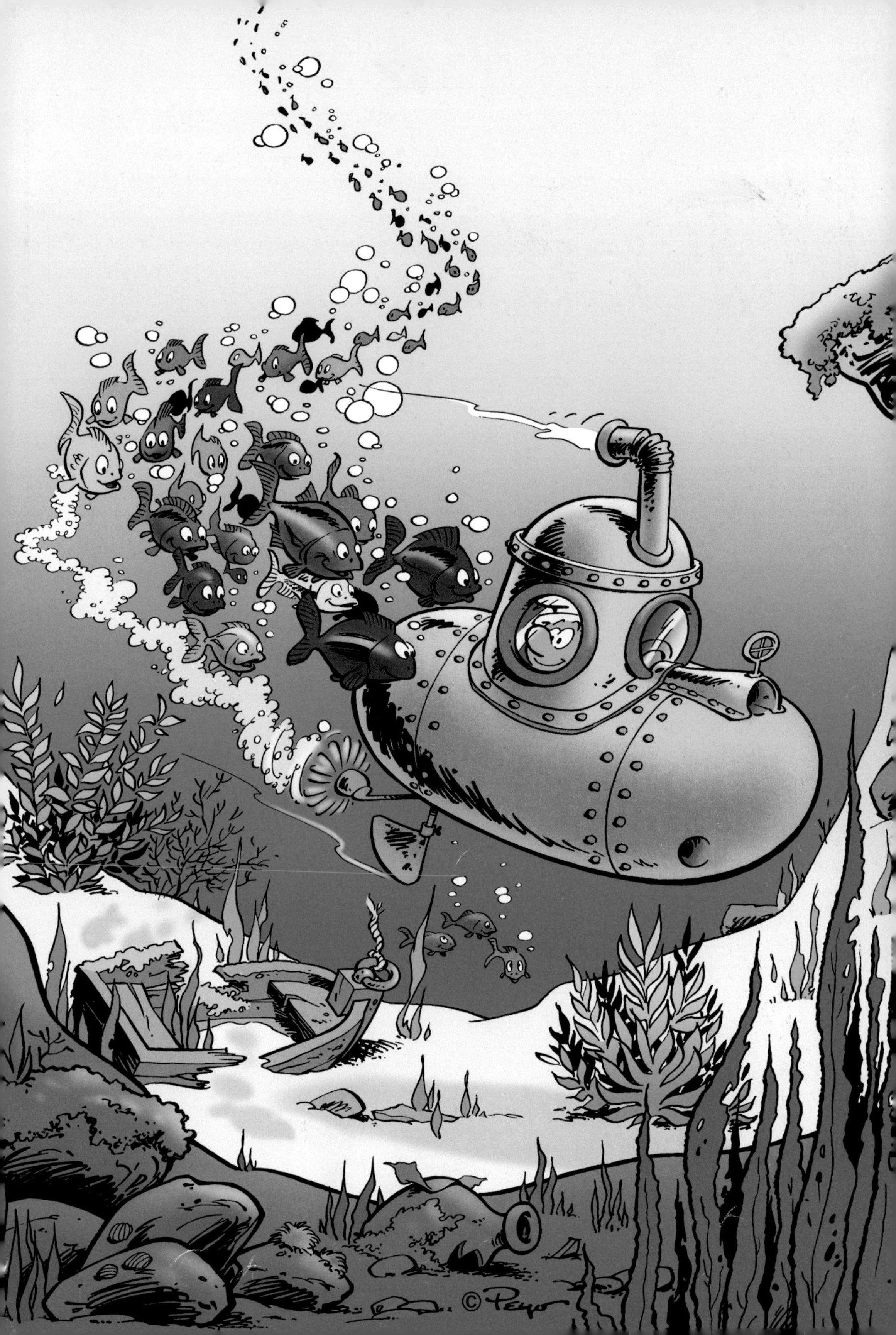
© Peyo

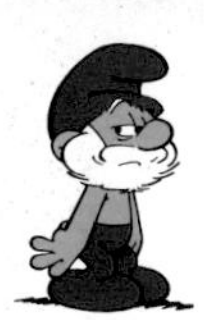

THE SMURFS COMIC STRIPS

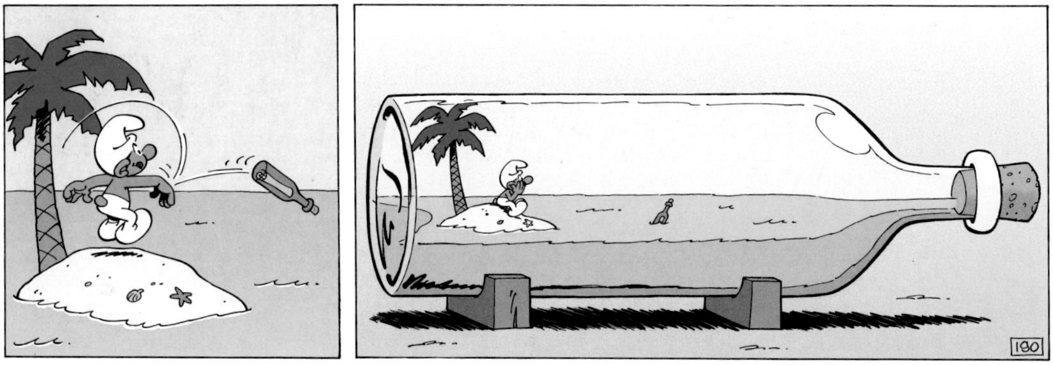
180

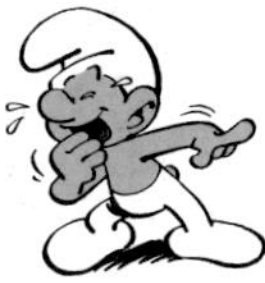

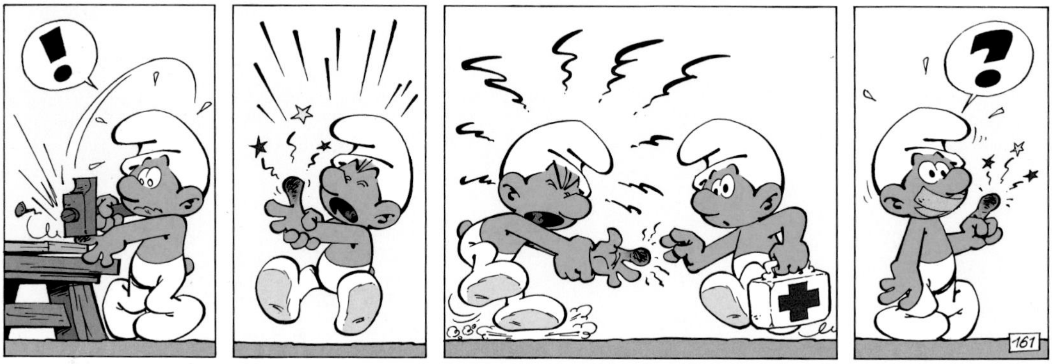
!
?
161

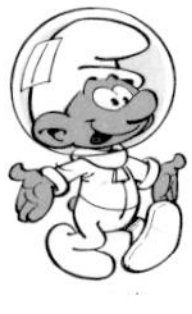

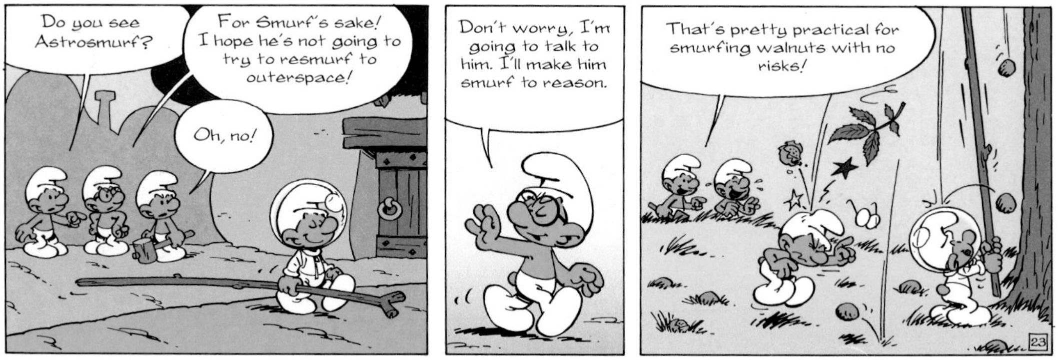
Do you see Astrosmurf?
For Smurf's sake! I hope he's not going to try to resmurf to outerspace!
Oh, no!
Don't worry, I'm going to talk to him. I'll make him smurf to reason.
That's pretty practical for smurfing walnuts with no risks!
23

WATCH OUT FOR
PAPERCUTZ™

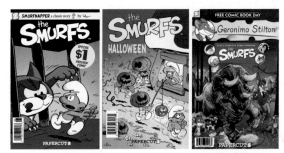

Welcome to the star-spanning, under-sea-faring, seventh SMURFS graphic novel from Papercutz, the scrappy, yet earthbound publisher of great graphic novels for all ages. I'm Jim Salicrup, your somewhat soggy Smurf-in-Chief, who is looking more and more like Gargamel as time goes on! Or, in other words, we're the folks who proudly publish Peyo's comic art masterpiece —THE SMURFS—in all-new editions.

If you're the curious type and you're wondering "who is this mysterious person known as Peyo?," then may I suggest you pick up Matt. Murray's new book, "The World of Smurfs," a celebration of tiny blue proportions? Not only is Mr. Murray our Smurfs Consultant, he's also America's leading Smurfolo-gist—his blog (http://smurfology.blogspot.com/) is a great source of Smurfs-related news and trivia. But if you really want an informative overview of the entire history of the Smurfs—from the original comics by Peyo to the new 3D motion picture—then "The World of Smurfs" is the book for you!

Speaking of history, for all THE SMURFS comic-book completists, we should mention the special edition comicbooks that we published to help gen-erate excitement for THE SMURFS graphic novel series. First, we published, a special preview comic for just one dollar—THE SMURFS Vol. 2, No. 1[1] in May 2010. Featuring an all-new cover, the special comicbook featured the very first appearances of Gargamel and Azrael in "The Smurfnapper," by Y. Delporte and Peyo. (Don't worry if you missed the comicbook, we'll be publishing "The Smurfnapper" in the Smurfs graphic novel #9 "Gargamel and the Smurfs!") Reaction at comicbook stores across America to the specially priced comicbook was predictably super-positive! Diamond Comics Dis-tributors made the comic a special "Featured Item of the Month," which helped get comic shops excited about it. THE SMURFS were back, and fans wanted more, more, MORE!

Working with Sarah Martinez and our friends at Diamond Comic Distributors, we also produced

a very special SMURFS comicbook for Halloween 2010. Cleverly titled THE SMURFS HALLOWEEN, this mini-comic featured two Smurfs stories "Hal-loween" and "The Smurfs and the Little Ghost." These comics were designed to be given away at Halloween as special treats, and most comicbook stores gave them away for free.

Speaking of free, Papercutz was invited to partici-pate in this year's Free Comic Book Day, which took place May 7th. We decided to go all out and create a special comic featuring a preview of our incredibly popular GERONIMO STILTON graphic novels, and as an extra-special bonus, we also included "The Smurf Submarine," which as sharp-eyed Smurf-fans already noticed, is also featured in this very graphic novel. Plus we threw in a sampling of the rarely-seen-in-America Smurfs comic strips (see page 54 for a few examples).

If you're really lucky, and you really, really want to include these comics in your collection, you can check with your favorite comicbook store to see if they still have any copies available, or if they can order some for you. To find the comicbook shop nearest you, call toll free 888 COMIC BOOK. But don't smurf it if you can't find 'em! All the Smurf stories in the comicbooks will be collected in the graphic novels sooner or later.

That's about all the Smurfiness we have room for this time around. Don't miss THE SMURFS graphic novel #8 "The Smurf Apprentice," coming soon! Stay Smurfy!

Smurfily yours,

JIM

---

[1] If you're a true SMURFS comicbook completist, we don't have to tell you that Marvel Comics published SMURFS Vol. 1, Nos. 1-3. As well as a SMURFS TREASURY EDITION, and a set of all new SMURFS mini-comics, back in 1983.

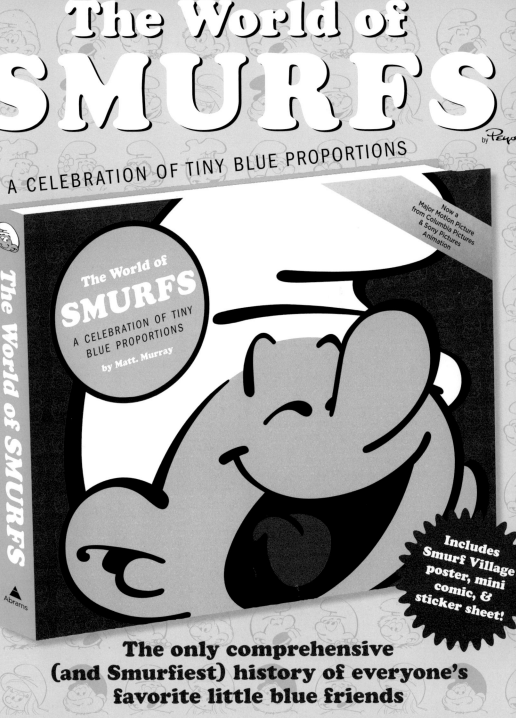

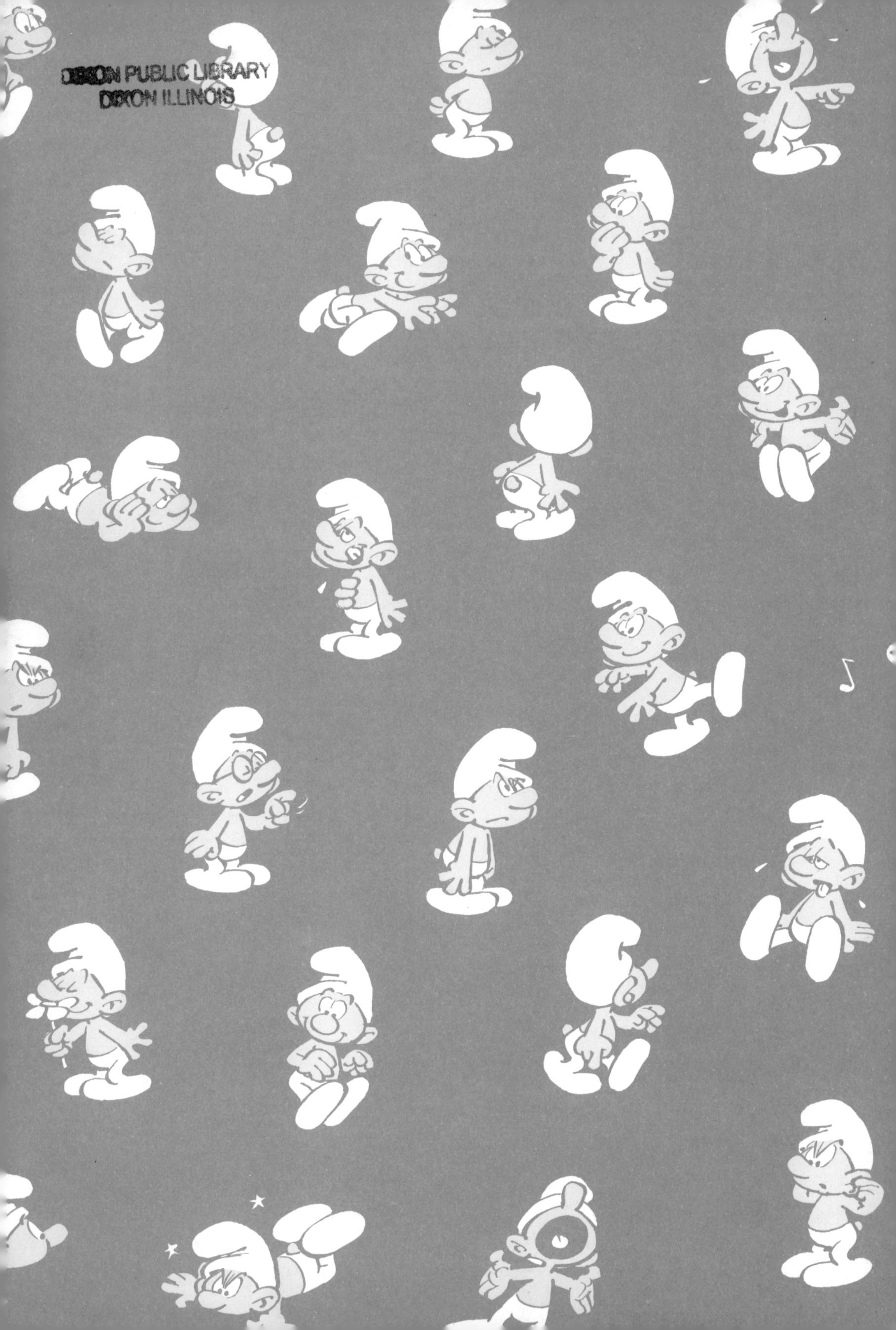